Ninth Standard at
Navjivan School

Also by Madhav Desai

Time to Kill and Other Stories
A collection of six short stories replete with
elements of mystery, suspense and surprise.

The World without God (Non-fiction)
If God does not exist, who is running our lives?

Ninth Standard at Navjivan School

MADHAV DESAI

PARTRIDGE
A Penguin Random House Company

To order additional copies of this book, contact
Partridge India
000 800 10062 62
orders.india@partridgepublishing.com

www.partridgepublishing.com/india

CONTENTS

— AUTHOR'S NOTE —

This story is set in Baroda in the '60s. It is no coincidence that I also finished my schooling from Baroda in the '60s. This has given me the advantage of being able to describe, from my own experience, the atmosphere that prevailed in the schools and the classrooms, and the mindset of girls and boys who had just entered adolescence.

Baroda has grown since then. A much larger proportion of school going children used to bicycle to school then, than they now do. You could buy a plate of snacks in the school canteen for 50 paise. People still used bulky cameras with film rolls to take pictures, and waited for two days after the entire roll was exposed, before they could see the photographs. Names and description of some of the places mentioned in the book have also changed over the years.

I have not modified any of these facts and figures to make them relevant to the present generation. I have a fond hope that this book will also be read by the next generation, and they may find even the modified settings outdated.

But this story is not about settings that keep changing with time. It is about the characters and their inter-relationships in a typical ninth standard of a typical school; and these are no different in the present generation from the '60s.

I hope you will enjoy this book.

Madhav Desai
31.12.2014

This book is for

Rekha
Devi
Rahul

CHAPTER 1

Navjivan School

Amit was out on his new bicycle once again. Mother had only asked him to go round the corner to buy a packet of tea, but whenever Amit got a chance to use his new bicycle, he would always wander off on long rides. He knew cycling even when he was in Bombay. But his parents would not allow him to ride on the busy streets there. Baroda was different. Here children even younger than Amit were seen riding on bicycles on the roads.

Amit would be thirteen next month. Tall for his age, Amit was fair, handsome and bright. About four months back, his father left his job in Bombay for a better post in Baroda. Mother was very excited about going back to Baroda, where she had spent her childhood. Many of her friends were still in Baroda. But neither Amit nor his younger sister Alka had liked the idea of having to leave Bombay, and especially their school in Bombay. Will Amit find a friend as jolly as Harish in his new school? And a teacher like Sunayanaben? Amit had been participating in every activity in the familiar atmosphere of that school. Would this be possible in Baroda? Would there be many activities in the school in Baroda?

Of course, Father had assured them that Navjivan School in Baroda, and its Principal Bhanubhai had a very good reputation and Amit and Alka would enjoy Navjivan School also just as much. Both children had good academic records so far and had no difficulty in securing admission in Navjivan School. Alka was still in the Fourth Standard, but Amit had entered the Ninth Standard, and the next few years would be crucial for his studies. Amit thought of his rival, Pankaj. Since the Fifth Standard, Amit and Pankaj had been competing for the first place in their class. The result for the Eighth standard was out just the day before Amit left Bombay, and he had stood first. Pankaj must have heaved a sigh of relief. With Amit gone, he would have no competition in the remaining years.

By now Amit had come quite a distance from home. This was the route that he had been taking very often when he went on his cycling expeditions in the recent days. He stopped his bike at the place where he always did and looked at the imposing sight ahead of him. Closed gates, cutting off entrance to a huge garden and a playground. Behind the garden, a magnificent building. And a board near the gate with the inscription: Navjivan School.

Although Amit had been here many times before, the sight of his future school brought a feeling of awe mixed with anxiety every time. Exactly one week later, when those wrought iron gates had opened, and the silence within was replaced by bubbling clamour, Amit would begin his new academic career with new friends and teachers who were completely unknown to him. Amit was unable to imagine this new experience, and was anxiously waiting for the school to open.

Alka was fortunate. Two girls living in the neighbourhood were in Alka's class in Navjivan. Alka had already developed friendship with them, and was not going to feel like an alien in the new school. Alka had also registered herself to ride by the school bus with her friends.

Amit suddenly realized that not all students in the school would be unfamiliar to him. Mother had recently come across an old friend, and her son Sunil was also in Navjivan. He was in the Tenth — a year ahead of Amit. Amit had met him very briefly, and he and his mother were coming over to their place in the evening. Indeed, it was for that reason that Mother had asked Amit to go and buy the packet of tea.

Amit turned his cycle around and raced back hurriedly. Sunil and his mother had just arrived when he reached home.

"Why did you take so long?" asked Mother.

"I decided to go on a long ride, Mom" Amit said, pulling the bike on its stand and locking it.

"Must have gone to see the school." Mother told her friend. "Both children are eagerly waiting for it to start."

Amit grinned at Sunil and took him inside to his room.

"Wow! Look at your music collection!" Sunil exclaimed as he entered the room. "You must love music!"

"We all do," said Amit, picking a record of his choice from the shelf and switching on the stereo. Both boys settled in easy chairs.

"Have you ever changed school in your life?" asked Amit.

"Never," said Sunil. "I have been with Navjivan right from the beginning. And Navjivan started with us. Ours was the first batch."

"I have also been with one school so far," Amit said. "I cannot imagine the experience."

"Let one month pass. You will not feel that you are going to a new school." Sunil predicted confidently.

"I don't know. I get nervous when I think that I will be surrounded by strangers on the first day."

"Haven't I told you that I will introduce you to everyone on the first day? What are you nervous about?" said Sunil. "Only yesterday Ketan from your class had come to my place. I have told him about you. Hemant also knows. By the time the school opens, everyone will know that a hero from Bombay is joining our school."

"Do you know everybody in my class? Who is among the brightest?"

"Ketan" Sunil said without hesitation.

"Did he stand first in the class last year?"

"That I wouldn't know. We don't have the system of giving ranks."

"Oh," Amit said, a bit disappointed. If he stood first at the end of the year would nobody know? Not even he himself?

"The rank is not officially announced. But everyone tries to find out the ranking by asking each other." Sunil explained. "Sometimes even the teacher is curious. Most probably Ketan had stood second last year."

"And who was first?"

"Varsha. She had joined Navjivan last year only. She is very arrogant."

Amit noted the names of Ketan and Varsha in his mind. "Who else is in my class?" he asked.

"Oh there are many others. There is Hemant. And then there is Jatin. Watch out for Jatin. He is a toughie."

"What do you mean toughie? He is not physically violent, is he?"

"Oh no. But he will try to bully you," said Sunil. "There are students in your class who are scared of him. But you needn't worry. He is my friend, and I will tell him not to bother you."

Amit made a mental note of Jatin's name also. "Any one else I should know about?" he asked, "What about girls?"

"Girls?" said Sunil, a little scornfully. "You don't want to mix with girls. Be careful. You will be teased to death if you go around talking to girls. Jatin won't leave you."

"Why?" asked Amit, surprised. "Don't boys and girls talk to each other in our school?"

Sunil shook his head firmly. "Bhanubhai and all teachers try very hard that they do. They will make a boy and a girl share a bench also. But that does not help. Some time back a boy from your class had gone to a girl's place on her birthday. But everyone teased him so much that the poor fellow had to change school and go somewhere else."

This experience was not entirely new for Amit. Even in his old school in Bombay, boys and girls did not mix very freely. But it was perhaps not as bad as what Sunil had just described. Amit himself had no problems talking to girls, and would often volunteer if any messages had to be delivered to the girls.

Sunil was talking about the activities in the school when his mother came in to call him. "I am leaving," he said. "Why don't you come to my place around nine on the thirteenth when the school opens? We will go to school together."

The rest of the week crawled. Amit was getting increasingly impatient. Sometimes, when he stood in front of the awesome school building, and thought about the things that he had heard about the school, he felt that the experience in Navjivan might not be very bad after all. But when he remembered his old school, and the good times that he had there, he was convinced that no other school could provide the same fun and excitement.

Little did he know then, how quickly, after the new year had started, were a number of exciting happenings going to take place, and how deeply was Amit going to get involved in each of them.

———◦❖◦———

FIRST TERM

CHAPTER 2

First Day at School

At nine-thirty on the thirteenth June, when Amit and Sunil reached school on their bikes, it was a different sight for Amit altogether. The school building, which was lifeless ever since Amit had seen it, had suddenly sprung to life. There was pandemonium in the compound, playground and the building and boys and girls of all ages could be seen everywhere, talking excitedly to each other in small groups. Sunil seemed to know almost everyone. Even on the way to the school, young children waiting for the school bus had waved at Sunil, and as they entered the compound, Sunil was caught up in a group of his class-mates, and Amit was forgotten for a while.

Two teachers were talking to each other at the entrance to the school building. Sunil saw them and took Amit to them. One of them, Sushilaben taught Gujarati in all classes from the Fifth to the Tenth, and was the class teacher in the

Ninth. The other, Jayaben was the Vice-Principal and taught Social Studies in the Ninth and the Tenth.

Both of them greeted Sunil. As Amit was introduced, Jayaben said immediately, "So you are the one who has come from Bombay. You will have to tell us all about your old school and its activities. This is your class teacher, Sushilaben. Sunil, have you shown him his classroom?"

"That's where I am taking him now," said Sunil and entered the building. As they walked along the long corridor, Amit saw classrooms on both sides of the corridor, and crowds near every room. Sunil's classroom was closer, and as soon as the crowd gathered outside the room saw Sunil, they called him to join them. Sunil was also eager to meet his friends. He saw one of Amit's classmates walking along.

"Parimal," he called the boy. "Meet Amit Divetia. He is joining your class. Will you take care of him?" Sunil gave a friendly punch on Amit's shoulder, and disappeared among his friends.

Parimal was tall, dark and wore glasses. He looked friendly and cheerful. Within minutes, Amit lost his self-consciousness and was chatting with his new friend animatedly. There was some time before the bell rang, and Parimal showed him around the school building.

"This is the Assembly Hall," he said as they came to a large hall in the centre of the building. "Every day begins with an assembly of students from the Fifth to the Tenth at ten forty-five."

Amit peeped inside. Preparations for the morning assembly were on. Two peons were spreading carpets. Near one end of the room was a table with three chairs behind it. There were flowers and incense on the table. In a corner, there were musical instruments.

"We all sing the prayer in chorus," explained Parimal, as he saw Amit look at the musical instruments. "Then there is a song. Sometimes Nirmalaben, the music teacher sings it, but more often, one of her students does. Mostly it is one of the girls from our class, Varsha."

Amit remembered Sunil having mentioned Varsha's name the other day. "Is she the one who stood first last year?" he asked.

"That's right. She is very clever. But she is equally arrogant," said Parimal. "How good are you in studies?"

"Last year I had also stood first in my class," said Amit, trying to sound as modest as he could, so that he is not branded as arrogant.

"Really?" cried Parimal thumping Amit on his back. "Terrific. What a competition it will be between you and Varsha!"

Next to the Assembly Hall was the Library, with racks along all walls filled with books and magazines. As today was the first day of school, there was hardly anyone in the library. Only one boy was sitting on a bench flipping pages of a magazine.

"That's Himanshu," whispered Parimal. "He is in the Eighth. He does not like to make friends with anyone, and spends all his free time in the library."

Across the corridor were the Principal's office and staff rooms. "I will show you the rear part of the building in the recess," Parimal said. "It is time for the bell to ring. Let's go to our classroom."

There was a crowd outside their classroom also, but Parimal did not stop there. He pushed Amit in the room. Amit saw that there were five rows of four two-seater benches in the class. The two files next to the door were taken up by girls. Amit had been warned about the tradition in the school, so he did look at them or try to talk to them. But he could sense that all girls had noticed him, and for a moment, the chattering had stopped.

Amit and Parimal sat on the front bench across the room. So far there weren't any other boys in the room, but almost immediately two boys entered and walked towards them. Parimal introduced them to Amit.

Ketan was a slightly built and sincere looking boy. Ghanshyam was also of similar build, dark and mischievous looking. Amit made friends with both of them almost instantly.

The population of boys was increasing rapidly. Everyone was busy talking to each other. Amit quickly stole a glance at the crowd of girls at the opposite end of the room. His attention was caught by a girl, who stood in the centre of the crowd, leaning against a bench. Her fair and attractive face, long hair and large eyes made her stand out among the other girls. For the last few minutes she had been talking very animatedly, and had captured the attention of all the girls in the crowd.

Amit turned his eyes away quickly. Three boys, who had been standing outside for a long time entered the room.

"Meet Jatin, Hemant and Dilip," Parimal introduced them to Amit. He turned to Jatin and said, "This is Amit Divetia from Bombay. He was first in his class."

"Isn't that wonderful?" Jatin turned to Dilip and exclaimed in mock enthusiasm. "We needed such geniuses in this class." Suddenly Jatin smiled at Amit and gave him a friendly punch. "Welcome. Sunil has told me all about you. You are related aren't you?"

Amit could not help being impressed with Jatin. He was tall, handsome and impressive. But behind the glasses that he wore, Amit saw eyes filled with skepticism that he could not fathom. Frankness and sincerity that Amit had found in the other boys were missing.

"Not related," Amit replied. "Our mothers are good friends."

At that moment, the school bell rang, and the crowds started to disperse.

"Sit with me for the time being," said Parimal. "Sushilaben will assign our permanent seats."

Amit glanced at that girl once again. She had taken a seat on the front bench near the door. Soon Sushilaben entered.

Everybody stood up. Sushilaben appeared to be very popular with the students, because as soon as she entered, many of them started talking to her at the same time. Sushilaben replied to some with a smiling face, and then brought the class to order.

"There are two new faces in this class," she announced. "I have met both in the morning, and I am sure you have also met them by now. But in case someone hasn't met them yet, let me introduce them. Amit Divetia," she said turning to Amit. Amit stood up. "Come here Amit, so that everyone can see you properly. And Namrata Patel."

Amit and a girl flanked Sushilaben and she put her hands around their shoulders. "Amit comes from Bombay and is very clever. Which were your favourite subjects, Amit?"

"Science and maths," said Amit.

"Not languages?"

"Languages also. But I like science and maths better."

"Once you start studying in my class, you will like languages also equally," Sushilaben said. "Do you enjoy sports?"

"Yes. I play cricket."

Sushilaben chatted with Namrata, and then asked both to go back to their seats. She started marking attendance by calling everyone by name. That gave Amit a good opportunity to know the names of the students in the class, although it was impossible to remember so many new names and faces in one day.

"Varsha Mehta," Sushilaben called. Amit straightened and looked at the girls' benches. The fair girl that Amit had noticed before the class started stood up.

"So this is Varsha!" Amit said to himself. "She is clever, sings well and is good looking too. No wonder she is arrogant! But I am no pushover either. Okay, I don't sing so well, but I play cricket, I have topped my class and I can make girls take notice of me."

After the attendance was taken it was time to go for the assembly. Sushilaben asked everyone to form a queue, and Amit noticed that Varsha and Ketan went directly to the assembly hall without standing in the queue.

When Amit entered the assembly hall, it was nearly full and there was a continuous stream of children coming in. Teachers had occupied their chairs. The three chairs at the head table were still vacant.

Exactly at a quarter to eleven Principal Bhanubhai entered, followed by Sunil and Ketan, and stood behind the three empty chairs. At once all the students stood up, and together, they recited the prayer. As the prayer ended, Bhanubhai sat in the centre chair, and Sunil and Ketan occupied the other two chairs.

At Navjivan, this was a daily routine, and was happening like clockwork. No one had to intervene.

Varsha entered and sang an invocation. She had a very sweet voice. Amit was not much of a singer, but he liked music and could appreciate good songs. He had to admit that Varsha could sing very well. And he also said to himself that she was a very pretty girl.

Amit unconsciously compared the assembly here with the assembly in his old school in Bombay. The assembly hall in Bombay was smaller and the students were more. As a result, all students had to remain standing during the assembly. It was not very practical to have more than a prayer and occasionally, some important announcements during the assembly session. Compared to that, this assembly was much more dignified and solemn.

After Varsha finished singing, Bhanubhai stood up. He wished all teachers and students a happy new academic year. He congratulated everyone for a hundred per cent result in the tenth standard last year, and insisted that the record be maintained this year also.

"I welcome all new students who have joined the school this year," he continued. "New students bring with them traditions from their old schools, some of which may be worth adopting. Ours is not an orthodox school, which cannot accept any new traditions worth accepting.

"A special characteristic of this school is that students make a significant contribution to every activity in this school. To plan and manage these activities, the students elect a Students' Council, the President and the Secretary of which are sitting here." He pointed to Sunil and Ketan. "The present Council was elected last year, and will continue till the next election that will take place in July."

After Bhanubhai ended his speech, Sunil rose. He wished everyone for the new academic year, welcomed the new students and adjourned the assembly.

As solemnly as they had entered the assembly hall, all students began to leave the hall, one class after another. Bhanubhai, Sunil and Ketan were the first ones to leave. When Amit walked out, he saw Varsha standing by the door, waiting to join the queue. As he walked past her, Amit felt an urge to talk to her – congratulate her for the lovely song, or just smile at her. But he was not sure of Varsha's reactions, and did not want to create a situation where the other students consider his behaviour strange. So he kept looking straight ahead, and came back to his classroom.

Sushilaben entered again and distributed the timetable. Studies started at eleven thirty everyday, after the assembly. There were seven periods of forty-five minutes each. There was a half-hour lunch break at one forty-five and a fifteen-minute milk break at three forty-five. The school ended at five thirty. On Saturdays, the school worked from eight to one.

"Now I am going to assign a seat to everyone," She said, taking out a sheet of paper from her purse. Reading from that sheet, she told each one where to sit. Each bench had a boy and a girl. As there were thirty-eight students in the class -nineteen boys and nineteen girls – this seating arrangement would work perfectly.

"Amit, you go there." Sushilaben read, and pointed to the last bench in the third file. As Amit gathered his satchel and started going there, a sudden wish flashed in his mind. Let Varsha be the one to sit next to him.

But his wish did not come true. "Purnima will sit next to Amit," came the next announcement. Amit saw that a plump, dark and tomboyish looking girl stuck out her tongue and with an embarrassed smile, started to move towards the last row. She was to be Amit's bench-mate for the rest of the year.

Varsha's name was announced almost immediately after this. She was to sit in the second file in the front row. A boy called Mahendra was placed next to her.

After taking her place, the first thing that Purnima did was to take her pencil and draw a line in the middle of the bench. Without as much as exchanging a glance, she had conveyed firmly to Amit that neither his books, pencil, clothing nor any part his body should cross that line.

The commotion created by shifting of places went on for about twenty minutes. After everyone had settled, Sushilaben said, "There is not much time left today. It is also the first day of school. So I am not going to start the lessons. Amit and Namrata will tell us something about their earlier schools."

Amit stood up and started to speak about his school in Bombay. He was in the midst of his speech when he heard the bell ring three times. Amit could not understand what that bell indicated, and he kept speaking. Suddenly he realized that something was wrong. The soft noise coming from outside the classroom had stopped abruptly. The students in the class had also become very still, and some of them had lowered their heads on the benches. Amit's voice was sounding like a roar because of the complete silence around.

"A very interesting thing about that school was…" Amit was saying. Suddenly he noticed that Purnima was stuffing her handkerchief in her mouth to stop laughing. A few girls had already started giggling. Sushilaben was signaling him with her finger on her lips to keep quiet. Parimal had also turned around and was also frantically giving him the same signal.

Sensing something wrong, Amit stopped speaking. The stillness continued for a minute. Then a single gong was sounded, and life returned to the classroom. Amit could hear more giggling.

"Amit," Sushilaben said immediately, "today was your first day, and somebody ought to have cautioned you about this. In our school, at twelve noon everyday, a peace bell is sounded. All students, teachers, peons and any guests who have come observe a minute's silence. They leave aside whatever work they are doing and preferably, shut their eyes."

"I was not aware of this," said Amit, turning red with embarrassment.

"Never mind," said Sushilaben, "But remember this henceforth. Everyday at noon. And you will soon find out that a minute's peace can do wonders."

Amit continued talking about his school, but his enthusiasm had completely shattered. Peace bell? What a strange rule! How many such new rules would he have to know about? And how many times would he have to suffer embarrassment because of such silly rules?

At one forty-five, when the class broke for lunch, Parimal came to him. "Let us go to the canteen," he said. "I will also show you the back side of the school building."

"Why didn't you tell me about the peace bell?" demanded Amit.

Parimal smiled as he remembered the incident. "Completely forgot. For us, it is an everyday occurrence, so we don't see anything strange or special in it."

Ketan and Ghanshyam had also joined them. The rear side of the school building housed classrooms for music and craft and a canteen. There was a large open area next to these classes.

"This is our open-air theatre," said Ketan. "All major celebrations take place here. For example, around January, we celebrate the Annual Day. On that day we perform plays and other entertainment programmes, and a lot of people come to watch the programme."

There was a queue in the canteen for snacks. "We will have to buy coupons first," Parimal told Amit. Ketan and Ghanshyam had coupon books from the last year, so they stood in the queue for the snacks, and Amit and Parimal stood in another queue for buying coupons.

"The coupon book will cost twenty rupees," Parimal said taking out his wallet.

"I haven't brought so much money today," said Amit with a start. Was he once again going to pay the penalty for not knowing the rules?

"No problem," said Parimal," You can buy loose coupons for fifty paise also. But I recommend that you buy the book tomorrow, so that you don't have to stand in this line everyday."

Amit bought a loose coupon and Parimal a coupon book. The book had ten pages, each with four coupons of fifty paise each.

Snacks consisted of *batatavada* today. After buying them they joined Ketan and Ghanshyam.

"How is your first day at Navjivan so far?" asked Ghanshyam, his mouth stuffed with *batatavada*.

"I have to get used to a whole lot of new rules," said Amit. "I am so overwhelmed by the new surroundings that I can't even think straight."

Ketan smiled. "Don't worry," he said. "Let a few days pass. You will get so familiar with these surroundings that you will feel you have been in this school from the first standard."

CHAPTER 3

Elocution Competition

June was coming to an end. Amit had started to get used to Navjivan School. He got to know of a few new rules and traditions of the school, but did not have to go through embarrassing situations again. For example, the school uniform consisted of blue shorts and white shirt for the boys and a blue pinafore and white blouse for the girls. But there was no dress code on Saturdays, and students were allowed to wear whatever they chose. Parimal had told Amit about this on Friday, so that he could dress appropriately the next day. Also, the seating regulations were relaxed on Saturdays, and students could sit wherever they wanted to. Amit had received timely information about this also, which prevented any embarrassing situation on Saturday.

The friendship between Amit and Parimal had been blossoming. They had been to each other's homes also. Amit had also developed close friendship with Ketan, Ghanshyam and a few other boys, and from time to time, received understanding and help from them. Amit found that Hemant and Dilip behaved like Jatin's henchmen. They were always with him, and hardly ever spoke to the others. Jatin himself was jolly, but for some reason, did not mix readily with Amit or his friends.

Amit also discovered that Ghanshyam and Purnima were cousins. In the class, they respected the tradition of not talking to each other, but outside the class, if they were seen talking to one another, no one would tease them. Because of their relationship, the boys of the class got to know if anything interesting was being discussed in the girls' camp, and the other way around.

Amit had to amend the impression that he had formed about Purnima on the first day. After sitting with her for two and a half weeks, Amit found her to be a jovial person. She wasn't particularly attractive, but Amit felt that if it was possible to make friends with her, he would have happily done so. Interaction between them so far had been limited to her asking Amit: "which is the next period?" or "what time is it?" on a few occasions. Once she had asked Amit her difficulty relating to a sum in mathematics.

But barring Purnima, Amit had not come in contact with any girl in the class. He did not even know names of more than half of them. The attention that he was paying to Varsha grew everyday, and he was waiting for an opportunity to draw her attention.

One day the Sanskrit teacher was explaining exceptions to a particular rule in grammar. Amit was feeling bored and was doodling on the last page of the notebook. He shifted his gaze to Varsha. She was sitting in the front bench, looking at the teacher, and Amit could see her long hair over her shoulders, a pink cheek, a shapely nose and a part of the eye. Amit was savouring her profile, when she turned back to speak to the girl sitting behind her, and Amit could feast his eyes with a view of her full face.

"Would Varsha ever have thought about me?" he mused. "Would she remember my name? Would she recognize me if we met in the street?"

Amit pretended to take notes of what the teacher was saying, and drew a couple of stars in the notebook, but kept his eyes fixed on Varsha. Suddenly Varsha straightened her head and her eyes met with Amit's. Amit recoiled as if he had received an electric shock, took his gaze away, and frantically drew three more stars.

"Varsha must have found out that I was staring at her," he thought, but could not resist the temptation to look at her again. After a few minutes, Varsha turned once again to talk to the girl behind her, once again their eyes met, once again both took their gazes away.

"I am sure I was caught this time," he thought, and kept doodling for some time. Then stealthily, he lifted his gaze. Varsha was still talking to her friend, her face turned. As Amit raised his eyes to look at her, he once again experienced an electric jolt. Varsha's eyes were on him!

"Was she really looking at me or am I imagining it?" he said to himself. "Or is there a smut on my nose or something?" He took out his hanky and wiped his face.

The Sanskrit teacher was so engrossed in giving examples, that it did not disturb him at all if the students talked with each other. Varsha kept talking with her friend almost throughout the class, and their gazes met so many times, that there was no doubt left in Amit's mind about it being his imagination.

During the lunch break, when Amit was sitting with his friends, he saw Jatin come towards him with a snack-tray in his hands. Hemant and Dilip were behind him, as usual.

"So Amit," said Jatin in a friendly tone, placing his hand on Amit's shoulder, "enjoying yourself in the new school?"

A bit taken aback by this sudden display of friendship, Amit said yes.

"We thought as much," said Jatin. "How many times did you stare at Varsha during the Sanskrit period?"

His secret was out, and that too in front of his friends! Amit turned scarlet with rage and embarrassment. "I don't know what you are talking about," he managed to say.

"Come off it," said Jatin. He pointed towards Hemant and Dilip and added, "the three of us keep a watch on who looks at whom and how often. So far it was only Varsha who was staring at you. Today, we caught you also." And the three of them went to their table, laughing.

Amit was looking so dumbfounded that Parimal said immediately, "Don't pay attention to anything he says. He enjoys teasing. The three of them have nothing better to do than make matches all the time."

But Amit's mortification and anger for Jatin did not last long. The feeling of elation was far stronger. At night while going to sleep, he closed his eyes and remembered Varsha's face, remembered the experience of the electric current that would pass through his body when he and Varsha looked at each other, and above all, remembered

Jatin's sentence: "So far it was only Varsha who was staring at you…"

He knew he had succeeded in catching Varsha's attention. He resolved that he would shine academically as well as in the extra-curricular activities in the school, so that he could strengthen Varsha's attraction towards himself.

As it happened, the very next day, Sushilaben announced in the class that an elocution competition was arranged for the students of the Eighth, Ninth and Tenth standards. The participants would speak on any topic of their choice for ten minutes. Those who wanted to participate were to give their names to the class teacher.

Varsha stood up immediately. "I want to participate," she said.

Sushilaben noted her name. "Any one else?" she asked.

Amit thought for a moment. His old school did not conduct such elocution, and he had no experience of public speaking. But he saw this as a good opportunity to kick-start his participation in the school activities. He also got up and volunteered.

From the three standards, seven students had registered for the competition. Amit chose the topic: "Does science bring progress or destruction?" for himself. When he talked to his parents about this, his father was delighted.

"I knew Navjivan School conducts a number of extra-curricular activities," he said. "I am glad that you are participating in them."

"I have no experience of elocution," said Amit. "You will have to help me."

"The topic that you have chosen was relevant even when I was a student," said Father. "I had also written an essay on this subject in school. Only, at that time it was the destructive powers of the atomic science that man had experienced. Over the years many more destructive powers have emerged."

"Like pollution," said Amit, "and global warming".

That night, after dinner Amit had a long discussion with his father and many interesting points emerged.

"If the human civilization on this earth were to be destroyed," Father had said, "evolution of a new civilization is impossible. Our civilization has used up so much of the natural resources for its development, that we have left nothing for the future caveman to climb the ladder of civilization."

Amit liked this idea very much and he noted it down. The following evening, he wrote an essay incorporating all these points. Father edited it and the final essay was ready.

Amit read the essay aloud twice. But when he tried to speak without referring to the written essay, he realized that he had missed out a few points. So he decided to memorize the whole essay.

On the day of the competition, the assembly ended earlier than usual. Bhanubhai asked everyone to remain seated, and he went and sat with the other teachers. Sunil and Ketan also joined their class mates. The seven contestants were given a separate place to sit. Sushilaben gave a brief introduction, and the competition started.

The first speaker was a boy from the Eighth standard. He was followed by Varsha. She went to the head table, and started to speak:

"Respected Principal Bhanubhai, teachers and dear friends. Today I will tell you why everyone likes Varsha so much." She paused briefly and then continued, "There are six seasons in India. Why is Varsha known as the Queen of all seasons?"

The first sentence had surprised everybody. They smiled when they heard the second, and immediately a rapport was created between the speaker and the audience.

The topic that Varsha had chosen was very ordinary, but the novelty in her thoughts, her presentation and her language were so good that she held the audience spell-bound. The speech came very naturally – she did not have to pause to think of the next line. She went through her speech with complete self confidence and was greeted with a thunderous applause from all teachers and students.

Amit was quite worried. He knew he would not be able to speak so well. Compared to Varsha, he found his essay dry and uninteresting. He took out the papers from his pocket to read the essay one last time.

After two more contestants, Amit's name was announced. He put the papers back in his pocket and went towards the head table. The size of the assembly hall and the presence of so many students and teachers made him very nervous.

He looked straight and started reciting the essay. At first he felt that his voice was trembling. His legs certainly were, but because he was standing behind a chair, he hoped nobody would notice them.

The first five minutes passed without any major trouble. Then suddenly his mind blanked out. He fought hard to remember the next lines but he could not remember anything. He scratched his head, cleared his throat, passed his tongue over the dried lips; but the next lines continued to elude him. He was conscious of a murmur that had started in the audience. "Looks like he has forgotten," Amit heard a Fifth grader in the front row say. With every passing moment, Amit felt more panicky, and the chances of his remembering those lines seemed to be getting more remote. Finally, with a trembling hand, he reached for the papers in his pocket. As soon as he had the papers in front of his eyes, he remembered the next line. He kept the papers in front of him during the rest of his speech. When he ended, the teachers clapped, but very few students did. Crestfallen, he walked to his place. He had to pass Varsha on his way, but he pretended that she did not exist.

There were three referees for this competition – one student and two teachers. When all speakers finished their speeches, the three referees consulted amongst themselves, and declared the result. Varsha was awarded the first prize. The second prize went to a boy from the Tenth.

Finally Bhanubhai returned to his place and addressed everyone. "Public speaking is an art. But it also requires courage. Only those who have stood here will be able to realize this. Those sitting in the audience will not appreciate this until they have had an experience for themselves.

"The prizes for today's competition were given to only two speakers: for their theme and their presentation. But congratulations must go to all participants – for their courage. I do hope that you will participate in all future activities of this school with the same zeal and courage."

CHAPTER 4

School Elections

As days passed, academic activities at Navjivan gathered momentum. Amit had created an impression of being an intelligent student in the class.

His class teacher, Sushilaben, was one of his favourite teachers. She treated all her student with equal affection, but she had identified Amit as one of her brighter students. Principal Bhanubhai used to teach English in the Ninth standard, and Amit's control over English language was the best in his class. Science had been Amit's favourite subject from the beginning, and he found that he enjoyed science even more at Navjivan. The Science class was held in a different room near the laboratory. The teacher, Avinashbhai, always carried out experiments in the lab to explain a scientific principle better. He also liked interaction in the class, and Amit played a leading role in this. So Avinashbhai was also very happy with Amit.

Mathematics was another subject that Amit liked very much. But Amit found that the standard of maths in this school was inferior to the standard in his old school. Almost everything that Mahendrabhai had taught so far was a repetition for Amit from the Eighth standard. Also, Mahendrabhai did not favour much interaction in the class. So Amit had not yet found an opportunity to impress the maths teacher with his talent in mathematics.

The rest of the subjects were Social Studies, Hindi and Sanskrit. Amit had no particular liking for any of them, but had no difficulty so far.

When the teacher was not in the class, Ketan or a girl called Trupti used to take the responsibility for monitoring the class. Amit knew that last year these two had been elected as the Class Representatives in the Students' Council. Each year, a new Council was formed and each class elected a boy and a girl to represent the class in the Council. The Council members then elected a President and a Secretary. This Council was responsible for all students' activities.

In the beginning of July, Bhanubhai announced that the elections would be held on the thirtieth July and those who wished to contest the election should give their names by the fifteenth of July. Everyone was so interested in the school elections that this announcement immediately changed the atmosphere in the school. In every class, students started discussing among themselves who would contest the elections.

Three days after the announcement, in the morning, as soon as Sushilaben entered the classroom, Jatin stood up.

"I would like to propose Hemant as the boys' representative in our class," he said.

41

"There is no such thing as the boys' representative," Sushilaben corrected. "If he is elected, he will have to represent the entire class – nineteen boys and nineteen girls."

Jatin did not seem to understand the difference.

"Is this acceptable to Hemant?" asked Sushilaben. Hemant nodded. "Then give me an application in writing," she said. "Who else wants to contest?"

A murmur rose in the class and two or three girls mentioned Varsha's name. Sushilaben looked enquiringly at Varsha, but she said, "No. I don't want to contest."

"All right. There is ample time till the fifteenth of July," Sushilaben said. "Consult among yourselves and let me know."

The next three or four days passed without any more students registering their names. On the twelfth, when Amit was sitting with his friends during the lunch break, he said, "No other boys from our class seem to be willing to contest. Hemant will get elected uncontested. Parimal, why don't you contest?"

"Who me?" said Parimal. "I don't have a chance against Jatin's candidate."

"Why?" asked Amit, surprised.

"Barring a few of us, no other boy will go against Jatin," said Parimal. "They are all afraid of him."

"But what about the girls?" asked Amit, "Surely, they will not vote for Hemant. Why, Hemant doesn't even talk to any of them!"

"I have an idea," Ghanshyam interjected. "Amit, suppose *you* contest? You are so handsome, that all girls will vote for you. Then all you need is one solitary vote from the boys to get a majority."

"How can I contest? I don't even know all rules yet."

"You only have to know the school regulations, not remember the constitution of India," said Ghanshyam. "Come on, the rules in this school are not so difficult to know. And we are with you to help."

"You are popular with both Sushilaben and Bhanubhai," said Ketan. "Even if you make mistakes they will forgive you."

"No, I don't buy your argument. What happens if all girls *don't* vote for me? I have already made a fool of myself by participating in that elocution competition. If I contest and lose, I will not be able to face myself in the mirror," Amit said. "Two years ago I had contested an election successfully in my old school. But that was different. I knew everybody and everybody knew me. In our class I cannot rely on the hope that all girls will vote for me. For some of them, I may be a complete stranger."

For the next two days Amit did not give much thought to this discussion. Friday the fifteenth was the last day for nomination. As the morning bell rang and Amit went to the class and occupied his seat, Purnima turned to him coyly and whispered, "Are you going to contest the election?"

On hearing such a long question from Purnima, Amit first jumped in surprise and then replied in the negative.

"But if you do contest, all girls will vote for you," said Purnima.

"What?" asked Amit, even more surprised.

"Ghanshyam told me two days back that they wanted you to contest. He asked me to find out the girls' reaction. I spoke to all the girls, and everyone told me that they would vote for you."

"Everyone?" asked Amit.

"All nineteen of them," replied Purnima.

Amit thought for a while. Ghanshyam's instincts were right.

"Who is going to contest from among the girls?" he asked.

"All the girls have decided to unanimously elect Varsha," said Purnima. "That girl over there." She pointed at Varsha just in case Amit did not know who Varsha was.

"But hadn't she refused to contest earlier?" asked Amit.

"She had refused to *contest*. When we assured her that no one else will contest against her, she accepted," said Purnima. "She likes to be given importance."

After the assembly, Amit had a brief discussion with his friends. As soon as Sushilaben entered the class, Parimal rose and proposed Amit's name, and immediately after that, Trupti proposed Varsha's name.

"Today is the last day for nominations," reminded Sushilaben. "If there are no more nominations from the girls, Varsha will be elected uncontested."

Most of the boys were very surprised to hear Amit's name being proposed. Jatin gave an angry glare at Amit.

No more nominations came up before the end of the day, and the election campaign started from the next day. When Amit came to the class on Monday, he saw Parimal and Ghanshyam fixing a large poster outside the classroom. The poster read:

> "Don't go by false promises
> Stay on you toes
> Vote for Amit Divetia
> Vote for the Rose"

At the bottom was the drawing of what looked like a pink sunflower.

"Where did you get this from?" asked Amit, amused.

"We made it yesterday," said Ghanshyam. "Like it?"

Amit's friends had taken up the responsibility for the campaign in earnest. Amit was glad that he had decided to contest. Instead of watching the excitement from outside, it was much more enjoyable to be at the centre of the excitement.

"The girls *are* voting for me, aren't they?" he checked with Purnima a few times. Purnima would smile in response and assure him that there were no defections.

Hemant had selected horse for the election symbol. His friends also campaigned for him, but as the days went by, his campaign appeared to have weakened. Perhaps they had made the same calculation that Ghanshyam had made, Amit decided.

"I have a feeling that Amit will get more votes than we had earlier expected," Parimal said two days before the election. "I was talking to Mahendra yesterday. He told me that he and his friends would also vote for Amit."

The election was on Saturday. Immediately after the assembly, at nine o'clock, the preparation for casting the votes started. Sushilaben stood in the classroom with the ballot box, and all students queued up outside and entered one by one to cast their vote. The ballot paper consisted of two names: Hemant and Amit. Varsha's name was not on the ballot paper, as she was elected without contest. Each student had to tick one of the two names, fold the ballot paper and place it in the box.

Attendance on that day was a hundred per cent with everyone looking eager and excited. Although there was no contest among girls, they were also looking very excited about the election.

Amit was among the first to vote. He naturally placed the tick against his own name. He felt excitement rising at the thought that Varsha would also place a tick against his name. He then left the room and joined his friends.

"I am trying to read the expressions on the faces of all those who enter the room to determine who they would vote for," said Ghanshyam. "My reading says that everyone has voted for you so far."

Once the voting was over, Sushilaben took the ballot box to the assembly room. Ballot boxes from other classes had also started arriving there, carried by the respective class teachers. Counting was to start at ten o'clock.

"No one except the candidate or one of his representatives will be allowed to enter the assembly hall," announced Vice Principal Jayaben addressing the crowds that were gathering outside. "The others, please go back to your classrooms."

The first part of her instruction was obeyed, the second was not. Students continued to crowd outside the hall, and teachers had to keep asking them to go back to their classes.

Amit went to the assembly hall. Hemant seemed to have disappeared immediately after the voting, and Jatin went to the hall instead. The doors closed.

Ballot boxes were placed on a long table. Behind the table, next to each box stood the respective class teacher, with one more teacher to help. Sushilaben opened her box and started to read out the name of the candidate marked on each ballot paper. Dineshbhai, the craft teacher stood next to her, counting the votes received by each of the two candidates.

The eventual result became apparent from just the first five or six ballot papers. When all votes were counted, Dineshbhai announced the result. "Amit thirty-three, Hemant five."

Jatin pumped Amit's hand, congratulating him. "I had known since long that you would win. Have a good time with Varsha."

Sushilaben and Dineshbhai too, congratulated Amit. Amit could not contain his delight. "Thirty-three versus five!" he said to himself. "That means most of the boys have voted for me. And of course, all the girls!"

What Amit found most exciting was that Varsha had voted for him. "Will she congratulate me?" he thought and decided that even if she felt shy, he will take the initiative and offer his congratulations to her. He was sure that on an occasion like this, she would surely reciprocate, and it would be the first time that they would have spoken to each other.

Amit prepared himself to face Varsha. It was going to be a big occasion. He ensured that his clothes were okay, took a comb from his pocket and passed it through his hair and cleared his throat. He then came out of the assembly hall.

Parimal was dancing outside. Dineshbhai had announced the result to the crowd waiting outside. Almost all the boys from Amit's class were in that crowd. Girls were not to be seen. Perhaps they were in the classroom, but waiting just as eagerly to know the result.

As soon as Amit stepped out, all boys were on top of him. Somebody thumped his back; somebody grabbed his hand and shook it. Then they all lifted him and carried him towards the classroom. A few girls were outside the class, and the expression on their faces showed that they were also sharing this excitement. The boys lowered Amit at the entrance to the classroom.

Standing opposite him was Varsha… smiling, moving gradually towards him.

Amit heard the sound of paper ripping above his head. Ghanshyam was emptying a packet of *gulal* on his head. Once again, the boys standing close to him jumped on him and rubbed the pink powder on his hair, face and clothes. Amit's eyes, nose and mouth were filled with the powder.

"Congratulations." Varsha said laughing.

Amit wiped the pink powder from his eyes. "Thankth," he said. His mouth was filled with the powder and he wasn't able to speak properly. "And thame to you."

CHAPTER 5

28th August

At twelve thirty in the afternoon, Bhanubhai had called a meeting of the elected representatives. Amit and Varsha went to that meeting. Amit saw that almost all those present at the meeting had *gulal* on them. Only those who were elected without contest seemed to have escaped.

Two representatives from each class from the Fifth to the Tenth were present in the meeting. Amit knew Pravin from the Tenth. The boy from the Eighth also looked familiar, and Amit soon remembered that he was Himanshu, who always sat in the library and never tried to mix with anyone. How such a person could ever win an election, was a mystery for Amit. Amit then realized that Himanshu did not have any *gulal* on his body. Did that mean he was unanimously elected in his class?

Bhanubhai started the meeting by congratulating all the winners and said that all the students' activities would now be the responsibility of this Council. In the previous years, all Councils had performed their function very well. Carrying on this tradition was the biggest responsibility of the new Council.

"The Council will meet on the first Tuesday of every month," continued the Principal. "As the first Tuesday of August is only three days away, there is nothing that I would like to say in today's meeting. We will only elect the new President and Secretary today, so that from Monday onwards, they can conduct the assembly."

To Amit's surprise, Pravin stood up and proposed Amit's name as the President. To his greater surprise, everyone greeted the proposal with applause. Amit hesitated.

"I am too new in this school to function in such a responsible position," he said. "Why don't we appoint Pravin as the President instead?"

"There is no rule that says that a new student cannot be the President," said Bhanubhai. "On the contrary, new students can provide new ideas that would bring novelty to the activities of the school. Secondly, we generally discourage students from the Tenth standard from taking on the position of President or Secretary. This is a very important year for them and they should concentrate on studies. Also, they will not be with us next year, and this Council will have to function till the elections are held next year. So more as a tradition rather than a rule, the President is from the Ninth standard and the Secretary from the Eighth."

Amit gave his consent for the post of President. Bhanubhai added, "and following the same tradition, shall we all agree to Himanshu becoming the Secretary?"

Everyone knew Himanshu, and nobody liked the idea of having Himanshu as the secretary. But since it was Bhanubhai who had suggested this, everyone agreed.

Bhanubhai adjourned the meeting, and asked Amit to stay back. The others left the assembly hall. When the two were alone, Bhanubhai said,"Well done, Amit. I am very happy that you take a leading role in the activities of this school. We expect a lot from you, and I am sure you will not disappoint us."

Amit was happy to hear this, but he knew that Bhanubhai had not detained him only to say this. He waited for the Principal to come to the point.

"How well are you acquainted with Himanshu?" Bhanubhai asked.

"Not much," replied Amit. "I have merely seen him a couple of times. He is not very sociable."

"Your observation is quite right," Bhanubhai said. "He is a clever boy, but has been a recluse from the very beginning. At the start of this year all the teachers had discussed how we could help him. His class teacher suggested that if he were appointed a class representative, he would be forced to take part in the school activities and mix with other children. Of course, Himanshu would have found it very difficult to contest and win an election, so the class teacher skillfully arranged to get him elected unanimously."

"I see," said Amit. The mystery of Himanshu's election was getting clearer.

"Taking this idea further, we had also decided to appoint him as the Secretary, so that Himanshu cannot escape taking on responsibility," Bhanubhai said. "Now, please do not mention all this to anyone else. But I thought that you must know the background, because as the President, you will be working very closely with Himanshu. Don't worry if Himanshu is not able to help you much. The other members in the Council are very capable, and you will find all of them very eager to work. Pravin, for example, can be an excellent support for you.

"My suggestion to you is that you think about the division of responsibilities among the Council members. Discuss it with Pravin, Himanshu and other senior members and implement it. That way, you will not have the entire burden on yourself. Of course, as the President, you are ultimately responsible for the functioning of the Council, but all of us have full confidence in you."

Amit felt very proud that Bhanubhai had expressed his utmost trust in him, and resolved to ensure that all school activities are successful.

The new Council took charge from Monday. In the assembly, there were five seats at the head table. A beaming Amit and an expressionless Himanshu flanked the Principal. Sunil and Ketan were also at the head table, for the last time. Sunil thanked everyone for the support received during the tenure of the outgoing council. Then Bhanubhai looked at Amit.

It was then that Amit realized that he would have to speak in the assembly. The elocution competition was still very fresh in his mind. This time Amit had not even prepared his speech.

But today he found new confidence in himself. Without any hesitation, he got up and said: "Respected Bhanubhai and teachers and dear friends. I am very grateful to all of you for the confidence you have placed in me by electing me to the post of President. On behalf of the new Students' Council, I wish to assure you that this year also, our school will be at the forefront of all activities. Every student will get an opportunity to associate with any activity that they have an inclination for. Of course, your co-operation will be essential for this, and I hope we will get it."

This little speech from the new President met with a warm applause from everyone in the hall.

After the assembly, Amit spent a few minutes with Himanshu, talking about the distribution of work. He had spent the entire Sunday thinking about this, and had decided that he would take charge of the cultural activities. Pravin had been taking a leading role in sports, and would take charge of sports and games. Himanshu would take the responsibility for the canteen. Most students used to go to the canteen, and this responsibility would help him come in contact with students.

Himanshu accepted the responsibility assigned to him. He neither expressed any enthusiasm nor hesitation. Amit had already had a discussion with Pravin. After obtaining consent from everyone, Amit spoke to Bhanubhai.

"It is a good arrangement," he said. "Ask Himanshu to take charge of the canteen from today. Both of you meet Manibhai before the lunch break."

Manibhai was the accountant in the office. He said, "We have given the contract for preparing the food to a cook. He takes the money required for the purchase of ingredients from me and accounts for it in the evening. So you need not worry about that part. Your responsibility is to distribute coupons to students and take money from them." He opened the cupboard and took out twenty books of coupons and forty loose coupons, and gave them to Himanshu.

"Each book is worth twenty rupees and each loose coupon is fifty paise," he said. "What is the value of the coupons I gave you?"

"Four twenty," said Amit immediately.

"Uh uh, I don't like that number," said Manibhai, giving ten more loose coupons to Himanshu, "So now you have coupons worth four hundred and twenty-five rupees. Keep these coupons in the table that you will occupy in the canteen. Here is the key to that table. Keep an account of the number of books and loose coupons sold every day. At five-thirty, give me the sale figures and the money you have collected. Make sure that you give me the account every day. Don't keep the money with you. Got it?"

Himanshu nodded.

"When the books or loose coupons are depleted, I will give you more," said Manibhai. "Now go to the canteen and keep the books and coupons I have given you in the drawer."

During the lunch break, Amit saw that Himanshu had started his new duty, working efficiently but without any enthusiasm. He went to Himanshu and asked whether he needed any help. "You will have to be here throughout the lunch break. Do you want to eat something?"

Himanshu shook his head, but Amit bought some snacks for him and kept them on his table.

At the end of the break, Amit went to Himanshu again. He was busy counting the coupons and money. "Are you enjoying your work?" asked Amit.

Without looking up from what he was doing, Himanshu nodded.

"I have never seen you in the canteen before," said Amit. "Don't you eat during the lunch break?"

"No," said Himanshu, "I read in the library."

"You enjoy reading? What else do you enjoy? Sports?"

"No," said Himanshu.

"Surely there must be something other than reading that you like," said Amit desperately. "Music?"

"No," said Himanshu, "I collect stamps."

"You do?" said Amit, happy that he could get something out of Himanshu, although he was himself not interested in stamp collection. "How large is your collection?"

"Fairly large. But I have too many stamps of the same kind. I have not been able to exchange stamps with anyone. Do you collect stamps?"

"I don't," said Amit, "but if anyone I know does, I will ask him to exchange stamps with you."

"Really?" asked Himanshu. For the first time Amit saw a glimmer in his dull eyes. "I would really like to collect stamps of many different countries. Do any of your friends have a stamp collection?"

"I don't know," said Amit, "but I will ask."

Amit checked with Parimal, Ketan and Ghanshyam, but none of them was interested in stamp collection.

***

As the month of August rolled by, students were getting more deeply involved in their studies. Surprise tests were conducted in almost all subjects. On comparing the marks with the other boys, Amit found out that Ketan was quite clever. Hemant was also getting good marks. Among boys,

Amit generally got the highest marks. But he had no idea of what the girls were getting.

Sushilaben had asked all students to keep a separate notebook for writing essays. She was checking the last essay written by the students, and so she had all books with her. One day when Amit and Parimal were passing by the staff room, Sushilaben called them, and requested them to carry the notebooks to the class. Amit carried some, Parimal carried some, but there were a few which were still left, and Parimal said he will come back and take them.

Both placed the lots they were carrying on the table, when Amit noticed that the top book in Parimal's lot was his. He took the book and saw the corrected essay. He had got fourteen marks out of twenty. Amit was satisfied. Not a bad score for an essay, he thought. Parimal had gone back to bring the remaining books and there was no one else in the class. On an impulse, Amit looked at the names on the other notebooks to see if he could find Varsha's. He did find her notebook, and quickly opened it. When he got to the last essay, he got a start. Sushilaben had given her eighteen out of twenty!

"Eighteen out of twenty in an essay!" thought Amit with disbelief. "What has she written to deserve that?"

Very quickly he skimmed through her essay. Her handwriting was very good and so was the language. Amit did not even know some of the words that she had used. He felt he was reading something written by some eminent literary figure.

Amit flipped the pages of her notebook and looked at the earlier essays. They all had the same neatness, the same dainty handwriting and each had consistently received very good marks.

"If this is the standard of her Gujarati language, I give up!" thought Amit. "And if she is equally good in the other subjects, who am I competing with! Compared to her, Pankaj in Bombay was a pushover!"

Just then, Amit could hear Parimal return to the classroom. Hurriedly he put Varsha's notebook with the other books. But the experience had left him shaken up. He knew that he would really have to work very hard to be able to compete with Varsha.

***

Amit had been in Baroda for four months now. But barring the school friends, he had made no other friends yet. There were one or two boys of his age in the neighbourhood, but except for the age, there was hardly anything else in common between Amit and them. Amit often had a problem of how to spend evenings and Sundays. Once the monsoon was over, he would start playing cricket in the school. But today, on the twenty-eighth August and Sunday, a constant drizzle had made the atmosphere dull and gloomy, and without any other activity, Amit was feeling very bored. That was the reason why he agreed to go out with Mother.

One of Mother's friends' daughter was getting engaged. Wherever Mother went in Baroda, she would always bump into old friends. She was sure that on an occasion like an engagement party, she was bound to revive many of her old acquaintances. She was really looking forward to it. Father had also decided to come, so all four of them set off by car.

The function was organized on a very large scale, and a lot of people were present. Father had found some of his friends, and so had Mother. So Amit and Alka sat in a corner, talking to each other, but beginning to feel bored, and hoping that their parents would decide to leave soon.

That is when Amit saw Varsha at a distance.

At first, he could not recognize her. She was wearing a sari, had her hair done differently and was wearing flowers around the hair-bun. She was engaged in talking to two girls much younger than herself. She did not seem to have noticed Amit.

Amit's mind wandered away from the conversation with his sister. He couldn't take his eyes off Varsha. He had never seen her in this attire, and had not imagined that she would look so beautiful in a sari.

Suddenly Alka asked, "Amit, isn't that girl from your class?"

"Who?" asked Amit, pretending not to have noticed Varsha.

"That girl over there…" said Alka pointing. "Varsha."

"Do you know her?" asked Amit, surprised.

"Of course. She has made friends with me," said Alka. She stood up and waved at Varsha, trying to catch her attention. After a while Varsha saw Alka first, and then Amit; and a pink blush rose on her cheeks.

Alka ran to her and called her to join them. With hesitating steps, Varsha came to them.

"Hello Varsha, what are *you* doing here?" Amit asked, wishing that he had dressed more carefully today.

"Imagine seeing *you* here, Amit!" said Varsha. "I have come with my mother. We are very close to the family of the girl who is getting engaged."

"My mother also seems to know them well," said Amit, pulling an empty chair towards him and indicating to Varsha to sit. Would she sit with him, or go back to those girls after this brief exchange?

Varsha accepted Amit's invitation and sat in the chair. "Are those girls your sisters?" asked Amit.

"Oh no," said Varsha. "Just acquaintances. I don't have any brother or sister."

Amit was wondering what he should talk to her about. Her excellent essay? No, he couldn't let her know that he had read her notebook. About the elocution competition? No again. It was too embarrassing a topic to raise. Elections? But they had already exchanged congratulations. About how well she sings in the assembly?

"You sing very well in the assembly," said he.

She smiled. "Do you like music?"

"I love music," said Amit. "I don't sing, but I enjoy listening."

"Those who like music always sing," said Varsha. "Only some people are too self-conscious to sing aloud and in public."

"I do sing in the bathroom," Amit admitted. "But only the four of us have heard me sing."

"You like cricket, don't you?" asked Varsha. How did she know that? Amit had said this in the class on the first day, but did Varsha remember that?

"Very much," said Amit. "I can't wait for the monsoon to get over, and start playing cricket in the school."

"I like to collect stamps," said Varsha. "I have made a huge album with stamps from all over the world. Are you interested in stamps?"

"I am not, but I know someone who is," said Amit. "Our Secretary."

"Himanshu?" asked Varsha with a note of contempt in her voice.

"Yes. He was telling me that he is looking for someone to exchange stamps with."

Varsha wrinkled her dainty nose. "I wouldn't go to Himanshu for exchanging stamps," she said. "Isn't he a very strange character?"

Amit also felt that if Himanshu had difficulty mixing with boys, it was too early for him to exchange stamps with Varsha.

"Have you settled down in our school?" asked Varsha. "How do you find it?"

"In the beginning, when everything was unfamiliar, I wasn't sure whether I would like this school. But now, I am really enjoying it," said Amit. "You haven't been in this school too long yourself, have you?"

"I came last year. I was with another school in Baroda. Navjivan is so much better than my old school, that I liked it from the first day," said Varsha. "Perhaps the only bad thing about Navjivan is the distance that exists between the boys and the girls."

"I agree with you," said Amit, "I wish something can be done about it."

Suddenly Varsha got up and said: "My mother is calling me. I think we are leaving."

Amit looked behind, and saw that Varsha's mother was standing with his mother. Evidently the two of them had known each other!

"Perhaps we will also leave," he said. The three of them went where both mothers were standing. Amit was introduced to Varsha's mother.

"So *this* is Amit!" she said. "Varsha can't stop talking about him at home. I didn't know he was your son!"

Amit looked at Varsha. She was looking at her feet in embarrassment.

"How will you go home?" asked Amit's mother.

"We will go by rickshaw," said Varsha's mother.

"Of course not," Amit's mother said. "It is pouring outside. Come with us. We are also leaving."

"Will we all fit in your car?"

"Certainly. It is just the two of you, isn't it?"

Amit's father had also come, so everyone started walking towards the car. How they were going to sit in the car was the question, and the arrangement that was finally decided was that the two women would sit in the back with Alka. Amit and Varsha would sit in the front with Father, who would drive.

Amit entered first, and as Varsha sat next to him, he shut the door.

"Everyone in?" asked Father, and started the car.

Amit and Varsha's shoulders were touching. Amit could smell the fragrance of the perfume and flowers that Varsha was wearing. He had not imagined that he would come so close to Varsha. He wished that he had also used perfume or something.

"Are you comfortable?" Varsha asked him, jerking him out of his reverie.

"Oh yes, yes," said Amit. "Be careful. Don't sit very close to the door. It does not lock properly."

What if Jatin or someone from his class happened to be cycling on that street, and saw them?

"How do you go to school everyday?" he asked.

"By public bus," said Varsha. "I would also have liked to go by bike, but my mother does not allow."

Parimal won't believe this if I told him about it tomorrow. But I am not going to tell anyone. Not even Parimal.

"Who is your best friend in the class?" he asked Varsha.

She thought for a while and said, "I don't have one specific person who is my best friend. It is not like you and Parimal."

Varsha's mother asked Father to stop the car near their house, and invited everyone in for a cup of tea. Amit was quite ready for it but his parents promised to come some other time, and they parted.

For Amit that melancholy Sunday the twenty-eighth August had suddenly changed into an exciting and memorable day.

CHAPTER 6

Mid-year Examinations

From the next day, as soon as Amit entered the classroom and saw Varsha, he would get a warm smile from her. But neither of them summoned the courage to sit with each other and talk as they had done on that day. Amit remembered that evening for a very long time. The images of Varsha speaking to him, her lovely face, her eyes, the movement of her pink lips, and the pearl-white teeth were etched in his mind. Her smile, sometimes frank, sometimes friendly and sometimes shy was unforgettable. When Amit remembered the soft touch and the sweet fragrance, he would lapse into a reverie. He kept wishing that he could experience these moments once again, with Varsha sitting close to him, talking to him and he looking at her and feasting his eyes.

The first Tuesday of September was on the sixth, and the Council met after the assembly. Pravin announced that the sporting activities were about to resume.

"All Class Representatives should announce in their classes that those who want to take sports as an activity should register their names with the captain of the sport they want to take part in," said he. Navjivan had many other activities besides sports, such as music and craft, but sports was the most popular activity. "Practice sessions will be held after school everyday. Our school has facility for sports like cricket, football and hockey, and there is a captain appointed for each game. It is the responsibility of the captain to prepare the team for that game. In December, we have competition with other schools, and we look upon the captain to take his team to victory."

"Who is the captain for cricket?" asked Amit.

"Jatin," said Pravin. "There are many students who register for cricket, so we have two teams playing cricket. The A-Team consists of the stronger players, and that is the team, which plays against other schools. The purpose of the B-Team is to accommodate more players and give them an opportunity to practice. Sometimes, when players from the A-Team are not available for a match, we select players from the B-Team."

Two days later Amit went to Jatin and expressed his interest in enrolling for cricket.

"We play with a season ball, not with a tennis ball," cautioned Jatin. He had a low opinion for clever students.

"I would not have been interested if you were playing cricket with a tennis ball," retorted Amit.

"Have you played cricket before?" Jatin asked.

"I was in the school team in Bombay," said Amit. "I am a batsman."

"Okay. Be present on the cricket ground on the fifteenth. But you will have to play everyday. I don't allow anyone to miss the practice sessions."

Amit went to the cricket field on the fifteenth after school. There were many others who had come. Amit gathered from the others that the students who had cleared the tenth standard last year had left some vacancies in the A-Team, but Jatin said that he would divide the players into A- and B-Teams only in November. Till then, everyone would play together.

Unfortunately for Amit, he got out on the first ball that he faced on that day. Jatin laughed scornfully, and ignored him for some days. But gradually, Amit picked up form and started showing his skill in batting and fielding, and Jatin's prejudice weakened. Amit played very diligently, never missing a single day.

Jatin was himself a very good player, but as a captain, he was very strict and quite unpopular. He would not tolerate if a player had to miss a session for some reason, and would shout and humiliate players who made mistakes in the field.

***

The twin responsibilities of being a Class Representative and the President kept Amit quite occupied. He got an opportunity to meet and interact with students of different age groups and classes. One day a girl from the Eighth approached him. Amit had noticed her during the assembly quite often. She was not as pretty as Varsha, but was attractive, with very lively eyes, which would light up when she smiled. Her teeth, Amit had noticed were uneven. She could look prettier if she got that corrected, Amit thought.

"When will we stage a play, Amit?" she asked.

"We have a play during our Annual Programme," Amit replied.

"And when is the Annual Programme?" she asked.

"Why, that is usually in the second term, around January," said Amit. "You should know better. This is my first year in this school."

"It is my first year also," said the girl. "I had heard that Navjivan stages good plays. I am very interested in acting. Will I get a chance?"

"It is too early to decide now," said Amit. "When the time comes, I will certainly keep you in mind. What is your name?"

"Bhairavi," said the girl. "I have acted earlier in my school plays and have also won a prize. Do you want to see it?"

"No, I trust you," said Amit. "As I said, I will keep you in mind when we are planning the Annual Programme."

***

Himanshu seemed to be attending to his responsibility with diligence, although Amit could not see any improvement in his attitude towards people. Amit kept checking with him from time to time whether he needed help, but he did not seem to require any.

One day Amit was having snacks in the canteen with his friends. The queue for buying coupons seemed a little longer than usual. Amit noticed a boy from the Eighth standard jump the queue and go directly to Himanshu. Amit rose immediately, went to that boy and said: "Do you want coupons? You will have to stand in the queue."

"I have just purchased a new book five minutes back," said the boy. "When I counted the coupons, I realized that there were only nine pages. I want to exchange this book."

Amit took the book and counted the pages. The boy was right. "Looks like the person who prints these coupons has made a mistake," he said to Himanshu, returning the book to him. "Keep this book aside, so that you don't sell it to somebody by mistake. You can give it back to Manibhai after the break." He then took a fresh book, counted the pages and gave it to the boy.

When the break was over, Amit went to Himanshu again, and said: "don't forget to return that book to Manibhai."

Himanshu looked at him with an expressionless face and said: "I think I have sold it to somebody."

"Sold it?" asked Amit surprised. "Hadn't I asked you to keep it aside?"

"I had kept it here, but in the rush, I lost track of it."

"That was very careless of you, Himanshu," said Amit, annoyed. "We have sold some unsuspecting person a book with fewer coupons."

"If he counts the pages, he will come back to change it," said Himanshu.

"And what if he doesn't count? Younger children also buy coupon books from here. It may not occur to them to verify the number of pages."

"If they don't realize it, why should we bother?" said Himanshu nonchalantly. Amit did not like this answer at all, but he realized that there was nothing that could be done.

Just as Amit was particular about efficiency, and hated such carelessness, he was a stickler for discipline. There wasn't anyone in his class who was rowdy or riotous, but there were some who occasionally indulged in mischief.

At noon one day, the peace bell rang. By now Amit was quite used to the peace bell and, indeed, had started to appreciate the concept. But whenever he heard the sound of the peace bell, he would remember his experience of the first day. On hearing the bell, he shut his eyes. Some students lowered their heads, supporting them on the bench. Total peace for a minute was very useful in sharpening the concentration.

Suddenly somebody sneezed loudly. In contrast to the silence that was prevailing, the sound of the sneeze was like an explosion making everyone jump. Some students giggled. Ghanshyam blew his nose in his hanky.

When the other bell sounded after a minute, Sushilaben said, "Ghanshyam, did you have to choose this moment to sneeze?"

"I tried very hard to control, Miss," Ghanshyam said still sniffling in his hanky. "But I couldn't."

This happened again the next day, and the day after. It was the Sanskrit class on one occasion, and Hindi on the other. Each time the students had a good laugh.

On the following day, it was Sushilaben's class once again. But a few minutes before noon, she had to go to the staff room to bring some books. As soon as she left the class, Amit and Varsha looked at each other, and Amit got up to monitor the class. It was a part of the responsibility of the

Class Representatives to ensure discipline when the teacher was not in the class.

Amit was standing at the teacher's table when the peace bell rang, and everyone was still. Very stealthily, Amit tiptoed to Ghanshyam's bench. He had lowered his head on the bench. Amit saw that he had taken out his hanky from his pocket, had made one of the corners stiff by twirling it and was pushing it in his nostril.

After a few seconds, he lifted his head to emit the sneeze. His mouth opened, his eyes narrowed, and from the narrowed eyes, he saw Amit standing close to him. He lost the sneeze, but his mouth remained agape.

As soon as the second bell rang, he rubbed the hanky on his nose, and smiled at Amit. But Amit did not return the smile. With a stern look, he kept staring at Ghanshyam.

"I was doing it for fun, my friend," said Ghanshyam, placing his hand on Amit's shoulder.

"I am your friend all right, but outside the class," said Amit gravely, pushing back Ghanshyam's hand.

"You are not going to report this to Sushilaben, are you?" asked Ghanshyam with a hint of panic in his voice.

Amit stared at Ghanshyam silently for a while. Then he said: "I will not, this time. But one more sneeze from you during the peace bell, and I will report to the Principal. Even if it is a genuine sneeze."

Everyone knew that Ghanshyam was Amit's close friend. This incident earned Amit the reputation for being a no-nonsense leader.

***

The mid-year examinations were in October. The timetable was announced by the middle of September. The exams were starting on the third of October, and were to continue for the whole week. For two weeks after that, the school would continue as usual and thereafter, close for Diwali vacation from the twenty-fourth of October.

The atmosphere in the school changed after the timetable was announced. Cricket and other activities were suspended, and everyone started preparing for the exams earnestly.

The exams started with Gujarati. When Amit was writing his paper, he felt that he was doing quite well, but he could not forget Varsha's essay that he had read, and kept feeling that she would be churning out literary classics.

The last paper was maths. Amit submitted his answer sheet about half an hour before time. He had had time to verify all his answers twice, and was confident that all the answers were right.

Amit could find out how the other boys were faring by talking to them. Perhaps he would have asked Varsha also, but during that week, he did not get an opportunity to ask.

The school returned to its normal routine from the tenth of October. All teachers had two weeks to correct the answer books, and return them to the class. Thus by the twenty-second, when the school closed for the vacation, all students would know the result of the mid-year exams.

None of the teachers had corrected the papers in the first week, but on the next Monday, Jayaben entered the classroom carrying the bunch of answer books. This sight had never failed to excite Amit – the teacher entering the class with answer books tucked in the arms, white strings tied to the answer books dangling, and the result of the six months of effort a few anxious moments away.

The practice in Navjivan was that each teacher would call the student to collect the paper, and announce the marks. Amit liked this practice, because this way, he would get to know his rivals' marks more readily, and monitor their positions. He wrote the names of some of his rivals on the last page of his notebook – Varsha, Trupti, Ketan, Hemant and a few others – and kept noting down their marks as they were announced.

Social Studies got him more marks than Amit had expected – seventy. Varsha had sixty-six. "Good start!" Amit said to himself.

But the situation changed on the next day, when Sanskrit and Hindi papers were given back. Varsha had scored more than Amit in both, and he was trailing Varsha by fourteen marks.

"That still leaves Gujarati," thought Amit. "But if the difference in Gujarati is not too much, I can still hope to outscore her in the remaining three subjects."

On Wednesday, marks in Gujarati and English were given to the class. Varsha got ten more in Gujarati, but Amit got ten more in English. Varsha continued to lead by fourteen, with the results in two of Amit's strongest subjects yet to come.

There was a mathematics class on Thursday, and Amit was hoping that they would get the papers back on that day, and the lead would be considerably reduced. But Mahendrabhai entered the classroom empty-handed, amid the protest from thirty-eight anxious students.

"Why do you forget that we still have one more class on Saturday before the vacation?" he asked. "You will get your papers back on Saturday."

Thursday was uneventful. On Friday, when they went to the Science class near the lab, they saw Avinashbhai standing near the table, with a bunch of papers on the table. Amit felt excitement rising in him. He had done very well in Science, and he felt confident that possibly today, and if not, certainly tomorrow he would emerge the leader.

"I am going to complete the portion that I wanted to cover today, before I start distributing papers," said the teacher. "Otherwise, there would be chaos in the class, and I will not be able to teach." He started to explain an experiment to measure friction, and for the first time, Amit found that he could not concentrate in the Science class.

About ten minutes before the end of the period, Avinashbhai wrapped up the topic, and turned to the answer books. Amit's name was one of the first to be called.

"I am going to keep your paper with me for some time," Avinashbhai said to Amit. Amit felt butterflies fluttering in his stomach. Had he done something terribly wrong?

"I want to show this paper to my Tenth standard students," Avinashbhai went on. "I want them to see how a science paper should be written. To the point, precise and scientifically correct. It is a very good paper, Amit. Congratulations."

"How many marks am I getting?" Amit asked, still holding his breath.

"Ninety-two," said Avinashbhai, and there was a buzz in the classroom.

Amit was flooded, first with relief and then with excitement. Will this put him in lead?

Not quite, he found out soon. Varsha had got eighty-one, and was still three marks ahead. Ketan, who also got good marks in Science was trailing Amit by four. The others seemed to be out of contention. Tomorrow was going to be crucial. Amit was hoping for full marks in mathematics.

The next day, when Mahendrabhai entered the classroom with answer books, Amit's heart started beating rapidly. The judgment day had arrived.

As it was a Saturday, Amit was sitting with Parimal. Ghanshyam was in the bench ahead of him. Ketan was a few benches away. Amit could see Varsha from where he was sitting. Would she also, like him, be keeping track of her rivals' scores? Was she aware that her position of lead was in danger today?

The first two papers turned out to be Hemant's and Trupti's. Amit was no longer interested in their marks, but only to complete the table that he had been maintaining, he noted their marks also. Hemant had beaten Trupti by a solitary mark.

It had all come down to how Varsha had fared in maths, Amit thought. Even if she got as high as ninety-seven, Amit could still equal her total, by scoring full marks in maths. If Varsha got more than ninety-seven, she would be beyond reach.

"Varsha Mehta," said Mahendrabhai. Amit held his breath. "Ninety-five."

There were loud gasps from some of the benches. Varsha went up to Mahendrabhai. "Couldn't solve one problem," said Mahendrabhai. "Otherwise, you would have got full marks."

"Is Varsha going to top the class this time also?" Ghanshyam turned around and asked.

"Don't be so sure," said Parimal, looking at Amit calculate totals frantically. "Amit still hasn't got his paper back."

"Are you going to beat Varsha?" Ghanshyam asked Amit.

"I only need ninety-eight," said Amit. He had meant to say this to himself, but it came out aloud. "Then both of us will end at the same total. If I get ninety-nine or a hundred, I will be first."

"Is it a hundred-mark paper or two-hundred?" asked Ghanshyam incredulously.

"Haven't you heard of someone get full marks in maths?" said Amit. "All my answers are right."

Ketan's name was announced shortly. He had got eighty-eight.

"Ketan is third," Amit said, totaling quickly. Ghanshyam showed three fingers to Ketan. "Hemant is fourth and Trupti fifth."

Amit had started to feel jittery that his name had not yet been announced. I hope my paper is not lost, he said to himself.

"Amit Divetia."

The earth had stopped spinning, Amit thought. The moment of truth had arrived. Ninety-eight, ninety-nine or a hundred?

"Where is Amit?" asked Mahendrabhai. Amit stood up and came out.

"Amit, all your answers are correct," said Mahendrabhai. "But I am not happy with your paper."

"Why?" asked Amit, a feeling of panic rising.

"Your method is not right," said Mahendrabhai.

"But this is how I have always solved such sums," Amit protested in desperation.

"This method might be acceptable in Bombay, but not here," Mahendrabhai said. "You seem to have done most of the calculations mentally. I cannot accept that, nor will the Board next year. All calculations must be shown in your answer. I have had to deduct marks in each answer." He held out the paper. "Eighty."

Amit was crestfallen. Eighty out of a hundred in maths? That had never happened to him before. And this time, all his answers were correct!

Amit returned to his bench feeling utterly deflated. On his way back, he cast a glance at Varsha. She did not notice him. She was busy counting on her fingertips, and writing something in a book; and jubilation showed on her face.

Amit did not have to count marks. He had mentally calculated that even Hemant and Trupti had a higher total. He was fifth in his class – and never before in his career had he finished lower than second.

Seeing that Amit was close to tears, Parimal brought his face close to his and whispered in his ears: "Don't worry. This was only the mid-year exam. The annual exam is yet to come!"

Amit looked at Parimal and gave a watery smile. He was a real friend, who knew Amit's feelings.

"You are right," said he, squeezing his arm. "The final exam is yet to come."

***

At night, before going to sleep, Amit looked back at the first term at Navjivan, and drew up the balance sheet. The result of the mid-year exam was an accident. He would be more careful in future. On the credit side, he had found a sincere friend in Parimal, he had acquired popularity and affection among the students, and above all, he had made friends with Varsha, the prettiest girl he had ever known. The difficulties that he had had to face in the first term were mainly on account of his lack of familiarity, but with all of that in the past, he would come out with flying colours in the second term.

How could he have imagined what the second term had in store for him?

———◦❖◦———

SECOND TERM

CHAPTER 7

Picnic

Winter had set in. Early mornings were chilly. Temperature would drop after sunset too. After the October heat, the onset on winter was welcome.

The second term at Navjivan School opened on November the fourteenth. After three weeks of silence, the school was once again bustling with students and teachers. Everyone was meeting their friends after a three-week separation.

This time, Amit was also a part of the buzz. When he had stepped in the school in the beginning of the first term, he did not know a soul. Today, the moment he entered the compound, his friends surrounded him. He met his classmates; he talked to the younger students, and also met the teachers.

He was eager to go to his class. He wanted to feel the familiar surroundings of the classroom again, but even more than that, he wanted to see Varsha. He remembered the last time they had met. On the last day of school before the vacation, he was leaving the school compound on his bike, when he saw Varsha and Purnima walking out. He took his cycle towards them, congratulated Varsha on the mid-year exam result, and wished both girls a happy Diwali. Varsha had returned the wishes with a smile. So had Purnima, but Amit's attention was focused on Varsha. Then they had parted.

He saw her after a break of three weeks. She also appeared to be looking out for him, because as soon as he entered the class, her attention was diverted to him. As usual, other girls surrounded her, but she smiled at Amit and wished him a happy New Year. Amit also wished all the girls.

In no time, did the activities at Navjivan pick up again. The timetable for the second term was a bit different from the first term. The studies ended forty-five minutes earlier. The last period was devoted to the extra-curricular activities that each student had chosen. Varsha would go to the music classes, Parimal to the crafts centre and Amit to the cricket ground. Some of these activities would continue even after five-thirty; although Amit found that with the sunset advancing everyday, the time for playing cricket was getting shorter.

About a week later, Jatin, with the help of Pravin, divided the cricket team into two. Amit knew that he played well, and if merit were the sole criterion, he should be selected in the A-Team. But he was aware of Jatin's prejudice against him, and so he kept his fingers crossed. When he found out that his name was included in the A-Team, he was pleasantly surprised. Mahendra from Amit's class was the wicketkeeper for the A-Team. Dilip and Ghanshyam were in the B-Team.

On the sixth December, Pravin announced in the Students' Council meeting that the Sports Day would be celebrated in the school on the twenty-sixth, the first day of the winter break. There would be a march past in the morning by students from the Fifth to the Seventh, followed by races. At ten, there would be a cricket match against Vidya Mandir.

Nirmala Vidya Mandir, or simply Vidya Mandir, as it was popularly called, was a neighbouring school, and competed with Navjivan in cricket every year. Navjivan played cricket matches with many other schools, but the match against Vidya Mandir was always special and more keenly contested.

For many years, Navjivan had been the winner, but for the last two years, Vidya Mandir had succeeded in defeating Navjivan. As it happened, Jatin had been Navjivan's captain for these two years. Both teams used to undergo changes every year, and so no one held Jatin responsible for their defeat. But Jatin had made it a prestige issue. This was Jatin's last year as the Captain, and a victory this year was very important for him. As soon as the match was announced, he doubled the vigour with which the practice was going on.

Around December – January, each class organized a picnic. The responsibility for organizing it was with the class teacher, but in the senior classes, the students usually took all the initiative, and sought the teacher's approval for the final arrangement.

In the first week of December, Bhanubhai mentioned about picnic in the assembly. The next day, after the cricket practice, Jatin told Amit: "All boys from our class have decided to go to Pavagadh for picnic. Tell Sushilaben, will you? And ask for her approval."

"All boys?" asked Amit. Why wasn't *he* counted among them? "Do you mind if I checked with them once again?"

"No problem," said Jatin. "We were talking about it during the lunch break today. You were perhaps busy with Himanshu."

"And before asking for Sushilaben's approval, I will also check with Varsha," said Amit.

Hearing the mention of Varsha's name, Dilip nudged Jatin, and Jatin laughed loudly. "Yes, do that also. It is a good excuse to talk to her."

The next morning, Amit checked with the boys. Jatin had spoken to all of them, and they had all liked the idea of going to Pavagadh. Amit wanted to speak to Varsha after the assembly, but before he could do it, she came to him and said: "After Bhanubhai spoke about picnic, all girls were discussing about it. We have decided to go to Vasad."

"Vasad?"

"Yes. It is on the bank of River Mahi, and is ideal for picnic."

"But we were thinking of going to Pavagadh,"

"Pavagadh?" asked Varsha. "But that is a very steep hill. Nobody would want to climb. At least none of the girls would."

Amit had never been to Pavagadh, and had no idea about it.

"Let me ask the boys about Vasad," he said.

"Vasad is a very good place. My aunt has a bungalow there, and we will have tea there. Everything has been arranged."

After the lunch break, Amit met Jatin.

"The girls are suggesting Vasad. They don't want to climb Pavagadh," he said.

"They can stay back, if they don't want to come," replied Jatin.

"That's not fair, Jatin. This picnic is for the whole class. We have to take their preferences into account also."

Ghanshyam intervened. "There is a place called Machi, half way to the top of Pavagadh. The bus can go up to Machi. It is a good place for picnic. Those who want to go to the top of the hill may walk up; the rest would stay at Machi, play games, eat and have fun. I don't think even boys will all go beyond Machi. I won't."

"Look, I've never been to Pavagadh. So I don't know what Machi is, how good it is, how tall Pavagadh is or how difficult it is to climb up," said Amit. "Why don't a few of us discuss with Varsha and some of the other girls, whether to go to Pavagadh or Vasad."

"That is your job," said Jatin. "You are our representative. You talk to them. All the boys want to go to Pavagadh."

During the next break, Amit met Varsha once again. "The boys are not willing to go to Vasad," he said. "Why don't you reconsider? They say Machi is a good place for picnic, and is accessible by bus."

"I won't go to Pavagadh," Varsha said firmly. "If other girls want, they can go with you."

"That is precisely what I want to avoid," said Amit. "Class picnic is fun only if everyone attends. Okay, I have a suggestion. Let's take a vote. If Vasad gets more votes, we will all go to Vasad; if Pavagadh gets more votes, we will all go to Pavagadh."

"I don't mind taking a vote," said Varsha. "But if Pavagadh wins, I will drop out."

We'll cross the bridge when we come to it, Amit thought, and after the cricket session, told Jatin about the decision to take a vote. At first, Jatin protested, but Amit was firm.

"Look Jatin, whether you like it or not, I represent the entire class – all the boys, *and* all the girls. Whatever the majority of students in this class decide, is what I will recommend to Sushilaben."

Finally, it was decided to take a vote.

Amit insisted on a secret ballot. If he were to ask everyone to raise their hands, some students might feel intimidated and not show their true preference. So on the next day, before Sushilaben entered the class, he asked everyone to put a chit on the table with the word "Pavagadh" or "Vasad" on it. As Amit had never been to Pavagadh himself, he voted for Pavagadh. When everyone had placed their votes on the table, the counting started. Amit and Jatin counted the votes, and Varsha and Purnima stood beside them to make sure that they did not cheat. When all votes were counted, Pavagadh got nineteen votes, and Vasad also nineteen.

"All girls have voted for Vasad, and all boys for Pavagadh," said Purnima, laughing.

"Let's have two picnics," said Jatin. "The boys will go to Pavagadh and the girls to Vasad."

Much to Amit's surprise, Varsha supported this suggestion.

"No, no," said Amit, "Sushilaben will never agree to this."

But in the absence of a better alternative, he suggested this to Sushilaben, when she entered.

Sushilaben got very angry. (She could never really get angry; but sometimes she pretended). "I am not going to accept this," she said, "Every year, all boys and girls from all classes in our school go for a picnic together. Why don't we have harmony in our class? What are the Class Representatives doing? If you cannot find a place that is acceptable to all of you, I will not allow this class to go for a picnic. I will have to recommend to the Principal to cancel the picnic for the Ninth standard."

Amit had no idea how to resolve this deadlock. He did not do anything on that day. The next day, at lunchtime, he was sitting with the other boys. Jatin was also there. So Amit knew that the picnic would come up for discussion.

It was Ghanshyam who raised the topic. "Let's have another vote," he suggested.

"What good is that going to do?" asked Amit. "Once again there will be nineteen votes on both sides."

"Maybe someone has had second thoughts," Ghanshyam said. "Maybe they have thought that if they didn't give in, we would all miss the picnic this year."

"He is right," said Jatin. "Do you have any other suggestion?"

"No, I don't," said Amit. "But I don't think his suggestion will work either."

"No harm trying it," said Jatin.

Amit tried to speak to Varsha once more. He wanted to talk to her when there was no one around. In the evening, when everyone had gone for their activity class, and Varsha was trying to locate her music book in the class, Amit went to her.

"Varsha, I think we will have to forgo the picnic this year," he said, "unless the two of us try and find a solution to this problem."

"I have a solution," said Varsha. "I am dropping out of the picnic, and I am withdrawing my vote. Now Pavagadh has more votes. You can all go there."

"But why?" asked Amit, agonized. "Why don't you give in just once? If you are ready to go to Pavagadh, other girls won't mind. We will go to Vasad some other time."

"Why should *I* give in?" asked Varsha. "Why not the boys?"

"I admit my failure. I cannot convince Jatin. All other boys are toeing his line."

"And what about you?" demanded Varsha. "You are not willing to give in either. Didn't you also vote for Pavagadh? If you had voted for Vasad, this situation would not have arisen."

"I voted for Pavagadh because I have never been there. I have been to Vasad."

"See?" said Varsha indignantly. "You wanted to go to Pavagadh, so you voted for Pavagadh. And now you are telling me that *I* should give in?"

Amit kept quiet for a while. Then he said: "All right. Let us have another vote."

"What difference is that going to make?" asked Varsha.

"I will vote for Vasad this time," said Amit. "I do want to go to Pavagadh, but I cannot see any other way out of this stalemate."

Amit could see from the expressions on Varsha's face that her anger was dissolving. "Will the boys agree to a second vote?" she asked.

"Leave that to me," said Amit. He did not mention that the suggestion had already come from them.

"And when Vasad wins, will they agree to come to Vasad?" asked Varsha.

"After the voting, we will tell Sushilaben that the majority of students want to go to Vasad," said Amit. "Those who don't want to come may stay back."

Now that an understanding had been reached, Varsha smiled at Amit. "Okay. We will have another vote tomorrow morning."

"Don't mention about this conversation to anyone," Amit stressed. "Not even the girls."

The next day, before Sushilaben came to the class, everyone was asked once again to indicate their preference on a chit and place it on the table. Once again Amit and Jatin counted the votes, Once again Varsha and Purnima stood beside them. Once again Pavagadh and Vasad ran neck and neck in the beginning. But towards the end, Vasad took a small lead.

The last four votes were in favour of Pavagadh. Pavagadh got twenty votes; Vasad eighteen.

The boys cheered triumphantly. Amit was baffled. Varsha cast an angry glance in his direction.

"Wait a minute," said Amit. "Let us count again."

The second count did not change the result. Varsha turned around in a huff and came back to her seat.

Amit could not figure out what had happened. He had voted in favour of Vasad. Was there a sleight of hand by Jatin or other boys? Or had *two* girls changed their minds and voted for Pavagadh?

Amit was glad that the impasse was resolved. He was also happy that they were going to Pavagadh. But he did not like the way Varsha had looked at him. "She thinks I have let her down," he thought.

Amit tried hard to meet Varsha alone, but he was not successful. As soon as the assembly was over, Amit went outside the hall so that he could call Varsha out of the queue going back to the class; but Varsha neither looked at him nor came out of the queue. She was with her friends during the breaks, and in the evening, went to the music class immediately after studies.

When the evening bell sounded, Amit was on the cricket ground. As soon as he heard the bell, he told Jatin that he wanted to have a drink of water, and ran to the school building. Varsha was coming out of the music class, and she was alone. Amit ran towards her.

She saw Amit coming, but did not stop. Amit finally caught up with her, panting.

"Varsha, I don't blame you for thinking that I let you down, but please believe me, I had voted for Vasad as we had agreed."

Varsha did not stop. She kept walking.

"Varsha, listen to me," Amit pleaded desperately. "It is obvious that one of the girls had changed her mind and voted for Pavagadh. Is it too far fetched to imagine that *two* girls may have voted for Pavagadh? Please believe me when I say that I voted as we had agreed."

Varsha stopped and stared at him, as if trying to decide whether he was telling the truth. "I don't believe you," she said finally. "You knew one of the girls had changed her mind. You put on an act to try and persuade me for the second round of voting. Please go away. I don't want to talk to you."

Without another look at Amit, she left the building.

*

At lunch on the next day, Ghanshyam was alone with Amit for a while. He asked: "Aren't you going to thank me, Amit?"

"What for?" asked Amit, and then he remembered that it was Ghanshyam's suggestion to have the second vote. "For suggesting a second vote?"

"For arranging to get more votes in favour of Pavagadh," Ghanshyam said.

"What do you mean?" asked Amit.

"After Sushilaben said in the class that if we cannot agree on a location we will have to forgo the picnic, I spoke to Purnima in the evening and persuaded her to come to Pavagadh. After she agreed, I suggested that she should get one more girl to agree for Pavagadh, just in case. The next day, before the lunch break, Purnima told me that she had managed to convince Namrata to come to Pavagadh. Actually, I was expecting two girls to have voted for Pavagadh; but perhaps Namrata changed her mind at the time of voting."

"Or maybe one boy voted for Vasad," Amit said slowly. The mystery of the second vote was beginning to unravel.

"Yes, of course," said Ghanshyam. "I didn't think of that."

"So when you were sure of having two of the girls' votes on our side, you suggested the second vote," said Amit.

"Yes," said Ghanshyam nodding. He was quite pleased with himself.

"Why didn't to tell me before the vote that you had managed these defections?"

"I didn't get time with you alone. And I did not want to say it in front of anyone else," said Ghanshyam. "Mind you, this is extremely confidential. Purnima agreed to vote for Pavagadh on the condition of complete secrecy. And she has told me that if anyone asks her, she is going to say that she had voted for Vasad. And I am sure the same goes for Namrata."

Amit thought for a while. If Varsha knew this, the misunderstanding between them would get cleared. But how was Varsha to know about this? He would be betraying not only Ghanshyam but also Purnima and Namrata, if he told Varsha. And in any case, Varsha was sure to check with Purnima and Namrata, and they were both going to deny.

Later in the day, Sushilaben approved the picnic to Pavagadh on the eighteenth. Amit wrote the announcement on the blackboard, mentioning that those who wished to attend should give their names and ten rupees to one of the Class Representatives.

Names and money from the boys started coming in from the next morning. No girl had so far approached Amit, but he assumed that they were giving their names to Varsha. During the second break, Trupti came to him, and asked: "Is it okay if I gave my money for the picnic to you?"

"Of course," said Amit, a little surprised.

Trupti gave him the ten rupees and said: "Varsha refuses to collect the money or register the names. She says she has nothing to do with this picnic."

Before the end of the day, most of the girls registered their names with Amit. The remaining students gave their names the next morning. Varsha's was the only name missing.

Amit had noticed that since the day of the second voting, Varsha had stopped smiling at him when he entered the classroom in the morning. She very rarely looked at him, and whenever she did, Amit could see a mixture of strange expressions in her eyes. Hurt, anger, defiance. Amit felt that she was deliberately trying to avoid him. Sometimes Amit wanted to meet her in privacy, explain rationally and try to mend their relationship. But Varsha did not allow such privacy.

The day after everyone had given their names, Amit steeled himself and during the lunch break, marched where Varsha and Purnima were sitting. Varsha saw him approaching, turned her face to Purnima, and started to talk with her.

"I had voted for Vasad, but you treat me like your enemy. Purnima voted for Pavagadh, and yet she remains your best friend. Where is your sense of justice?" Amit felt like telling her; but didn't. Instead, he said: "Varsha, I haven't received your name for the picnic."

"I am not coming," Varsha said, her voice cold. "You know that."

"But Varsha…" Amit stared.

Varsha cut him short. "My aunt and my cousin are coming to my place on that day," she said. "I will not be able to come to your picnic."

This was an excuse. Amit knew it.

"And your aunt and your cousin would not have come to your place if we had decided to go to Vasad. Isn't that right?"

"We haven't decided to go to Vasad. So the question does not arise," said Varsha.

Purnima had been listening to this exchange silently. As they went back to the class and took their seats, she told Amit: "It was a good try. But she will not change her mind so easily."

"If what you mean is that there are some difficult ways to make her reconsider, I will try those also," said Amit.

"Only if we change our plans and go to Vasad will she reconsider."

"But how is that possible? After everything has been decided, we can't change our plans just because one person is adamant about it."

"She still believes that we will do it," said Purnima. "She thinks we will not enjoy the picnic without her, and will do whatever she wants in order to have her join us."

"That is out of the question," said Amit.

"I know. But she doesn't."

As the eighteenth drew nearer, all the students started discussing the plans for the picnic. There were discussions about which snacks to bring and which games to carry. There were discussions about when the bus would leave, when it would reach Machi, and when it would come back. There were discussions about where to camp, what to do throughout the day, and whether to climb up to the top. Every student joined these discussions excitedly. Only Varsha took no interest in them at all.

"If Varsha believes that *we* will not have fun without her," said Amit to Purnima one day, "does she realize what *she* is missing?"

"Even now, she is ready to come to the picnic," said Purnima.

"Then what is stopping her?" asked Amit. "I will accept her name even today. Never mind if the last date is over."

"But she will come only on her condition," said Purnima. "Vasad."

Amit sighed in exasperation. "At first all girls wanted Vasad. But now everyone is happy to go to Pavagadh. If Varsha also agrees for Pavagadh, would she get six inches shorter?"

Purnima laughed heartily. "You don't know her," she said.

Amit dropped the idea of trying to persuade Varsha. He was feeling unhappy about the way Varsha was behaving with him, but he thought that once the picnic was a thing of the past, the misunderstanding between them would also be forgotten, and everything would be as before.

Sunday the eighteenth turned out to be an ideal day for picnic. The morning was cooler than usual, and everybody was dressed in woollens when they assembled in the school compound. The bus had also arrived on time.

Sushilaben and Dineshbhai were going to join the class in the picnic. Dineshbhai, the craft teacher, was very popular among the students of the class. With thirty-seven students and two teachers, the bus set off for Pavagadh.

The bus could go up to Machi, which was half way up the hill. Arrangement was made with a holiday home in Machi for the day's stay and food. After tea and snacks at the holiday home, about eight boys and three girls decided to walk up to the top of the hill. Amit and all his friends were among those who stayed at Machi.

The inhibition that prevailed between the boys and the girls in the classroom gradually started dissolving, and very soon disappeared completely. Together they played games, sang songs, and once again played games. Amit found out that Trupti was also a good singer. Namrata, who was very shy and quiet in the class, was so good at mimicking accents of people from different parts of Gujarat that everyone had cramps in their stomachs from laughing. Purnima delivered dialogues from films in the style of the film actors. Parimal and Ghanshyam kept coming in with jokes. Then everyone asked Amit to sing. At first, Amit refused, but when everyone insisted, he sang a duet from a recent film with Trupti.

Amit was very popular with the girls from his class. Amit did suspect this, but today, he knew it without doubt. Everybody paid most attention to him when he spoke, laughed most when he joked, applauded most when he sang.

Parimal had brought a portable music system with him. When they got tired of their own performance, he switched on the system and put on the latest numbers in pop music. "Let's dance," said Ghanshyam and started wiggling most clumsily. Fortunately, other boys and girls, some of them very graceful, joined in immediately.

Sushilaben and Dineshbhai were thoroughly enjoying themselves. They had become one with the group of students, and participated in all the activities. Today, they behaved not like teachers, but more like friends, and felt a lot younger too. Earlier, Sushilaben had sung a song, and although she refused to join the dance, Dineshbhai enjoyed dancing to the pop music with the others.

Purnima was carrying a camera, and had kept clicking throughout the get-together. They played many different games. They played the Blind Man's buff, they played kho-kho, two boys wrestled; and they were all very hungry. The group that had gone to the top of the hill returned quite late. They had their lunch late in the afternoon, played some more, sang some more, and after sunset, started the return journey.

Around eight-thirty, the bus entered the school compound, with boys and girls still laughing, still singing, but so tired that they kept falling over each other. With hurrahs and cheers, they all separated. The picnic of the Ninth standard was an unqualified success.

Amit had missed Varsha every moment of that day.

———⋯◆⋯———

CHAPTER 8

Cricket Match

No one spoke of anything other than the picnic the next day. Everyone kept remembering the fun they had had, and talked about things they had enjoyed most.

"You should have come to the top of the hill," said Mahendra, who was among the climbers. "The view from there was too good."

"Who would have imagined that Dineshbhai dances so gracefully?" Amit heard Trupti say to Purnima before the class started.

"Varsha, I wish you could have joined us," said Namrata. Most girls were under the impression that Varsha did not come because she had guests that day. "You really missed something."

Varsha did not like all this. She did not like it at all. At lunch when she was passing by the boys, she saw Parimal thump Amit on his back, and laugh loudly, remembering an incident of yesterday. Everyone seems to have had fun, she thought grimly. Even without me.

Two days later, Purnima brought the photographs that she had taken during the picnic. Either she was a very talented photographer, or her camera was very good; but the snaps had come out remarkably well. In more than half the photos, Amit featured prominently. In one, he had tied a hanky over his eyes, and was groping at Vandana's face; and the girl was giggling ecstatically. In another, he was dancing with Trupti and Namrata. Purnima passed the photos around. They also reached Varsha, but she pretended not to be interested and passed them on without seeing. In reality, of course, she had peeked at them many times while they were with someone else. She tried hard to suppress her anger and jealousy and behave as normally as possible with the other girls.

For Amit, Jatin and a few other boys, the picnic soon went into the background, as they had to turn their focus to cricket. The match with Vidya Mandir was on Monday. Jatin had been concentrating hard on the A-Team, and was quite satisfied with the state of readiness of the team. If everyone played in the match the way they were playing during the practice sessions, he felt confident of their victory. Their fielding was a bit weak, and the bowlers could do with some more practice, but on the whole, things seemed to be fine.

Until Friday.

On Friday, everything went topsy-turvy. Why Friday's events did not take place earlier was a mystery. Jatin had the habit of shouting at players who did not play well, and no one liked that. As the crucial day approached, Jatin started getting tenser, and his tantrums increased. On Friday, four players became the target of Jatin's foul mood. Rajesh was absent on Thursday without informing Jatin, Rohit came late on Friday, and Deepak and Gaurang did not field with agility. Gaurang also dropped an easy catch.

When the play ended on Friday, Jatin told everyone: "I am still not satisfied. We will play on Saturday and Sunday."

"I won't be able to come over the week-end," said Deepak, still sore at the humiliation meted out by Jatin earlier in the evening.

"Why?" demanded Jatin. "Have you forgotten that we have the match on Monday?"

"Who's talking about Monday?" Deepak shot back. "I said I won't be coming on Saturday and Sunday."

"I want the practice to continue on Saturday and Sunday," said Jatin. "If you want to play on Monday, you'd better be present over the week end."

"Are you telling me that if I don't come over the week end, you will drop me from the team?" asked Deepak.

"Do you have any doubt in your mind?" asked Jatin, flaring up. "I am telling everyone here as the captain of this team. We are going to practice over this week end, and I want everyone to attend the practice sessions."

"I will also not be able to come over this week end," said Gaurang. Rajesh and Rohit also asked to be excused from the week end practice.

Jatin bit his lips and glared at the four rebels. They were the top batsmen of the A-Team.

"Let me repeat," he said slowly but firmly. "I want the team to have more practice before the match. Those who want to be included in the match will attend the practice sessions."

"We are not coming over this week end," said Rohit, with the same firmness. "Kick us out of the team if that is what you want. We have been practicing hard for the last few weeks, and I know we are playing well. We don't need more practice."

"That is for me to decide," snapped Jatin. "I am the captain, and I am responsible for preparing the team for the match."

"Jatin, cool down," Pravin started, but Jatin cut him short.

"We will assemble here at one o'clock tomorrow afternoon," he said. "Those who are not present will sit in the spectators' tent on Monday."

He stormed out of the field and went into the building. Pravin and Amit followed him.

"Jatin, don't get so excited," said Pravin, as they stood in the corridor. "You know as well as I do, that we will not be able to play the match without those four."

"Why not?" asked Jatin.

"Because they are our best batsmen," said Pravin.

"What do you mean they are the best batsmen? Am I not going to play? Aren't you playing? Isn't this Amit playing?"

"But have you considered the strength of our opponents?" asked Pravin. "Without our best team, we have no chance of winning. What do you say, Amit?"

"What has Amit got to do with this?" said Jatin. "I am the captain."

"But I am responsible for the sporting activities of the school," reminded Pravin, "and Amit is the President of the Council."

"Then dismiss me as the captain," said Jatin. "But as long as you have entrusted captaincy to me, I will lay down the ground rules."

"Jatin is quite right," said Amit, unexpectedly. "If these players don't listen to the captain today, what is the assurance that they will obey him during the match?"

Jatin was both surprised and happy at this unexpected support from Amit.

"If that is how you also feel, I have nothing else to say," said Pravin. "But whom are we going to include in place of these four?"

"There are some batsmen with good potential in the B-Team," said Amit. "Let us try and identify them."

"No one in the B-Team will come anywhere close to the four batsmen that we are losing," said Pravin. "Our batting will be extremely weakened."

"You, Jatin, Vikram and I – four of us will try and bat as well as we can," said Amit. "We also have good bowlers in our side. I don't think we should give up hope completely."

Jatin had taken out the list of players in the B-Team from his pocket. "Dilip, Ghanshyam, Prakash and Jitendra," he said, reading from that list. "I will ask these four to be present tomorrow. We will fill whatever vacancies that exist in our team from these four."

On Saturday, everybody waited till one-thirty. None of the rebellious players had turned up. The four players from the B-Team had come very enthusiastically, expecting a big break in their cricketing career. At one-thirty, Jatin announced the team that would play in the match against Vidya Mandir on Monday. He had omitted Rohit, Rajesh, Deepak and Gaurang, and in their place, he had included

Dilip, Ghanshyam, Prakash and Jitendra. Everyone practiced diligently on Saturday and Sunday. All four new players were looking weak for the big match and Jatin had started to get worried, but he did not express his concern.

Although the school had closed for a one-week winter break, students and teachers of all classes and many parents had turned up on Monday morning. At seven-thirty, the sports day celebration started with a march past by the younger students. That was followed by races and different competitions for them. At nine-thirty, the students of Vidya Mandir arrived.

On the playground, two tents were erected opposite each other. In one of them, players from Navjivan, other students, teachers and parents were sitting. The other tent was meant for Vidya Mandir, and had a very large number of spectators too. Varsha was sitting with her friends, dressed in a white Punjabi dress and dark glasses. As always, she looked very attractive, and Amit had a strong feeling of remorse for the way their friendship had been affected. She was busy talking to her friends, and did not even notice Amit.

"She will have to take notice of me when I am batting," Amit consoled himself. "I am sure I will impress her with my performance today."

The four rebels had turned up in the morning, dressed in the cricketing clothes. When they found out that their names were not in the final team, they couldn't believe it.

"What is Jatin up to?" asked Deepak incredulously, "He has replaced us with four players from the B-Team! This year we will lose to Vidya Mandir even more badly!"

They debated whether to stay on to see the match or not. All of them were keen to see the match, so they went and sat in

Navjivan's tent. They should really have sat in Vidya Mandir's tent, because they were keen to see Navjivan lose today.

Jatin won the toss, and decided to field first. Both teams were going to play forty overs each, and the team to score more runs in forty overs would win.

At ten, Jatin lead his team out of the tent, and everyone in the tent clapped in encouragement. "Show it to them, Jatin," somebody shouted.

A Parsee boy named Jamshed was going to open the bowling for Navjivan. Jatin, Pravin and Vikram were also good bowlers for Navjivan. Ghanshyam could also bowl.

"Our bowling and fielding must be top class," Jatin told the players. "Our batting may not be as strong as we want it to be; so let us chase as small a target as possible."

Vidya Mandir's captain Jagadish and Kishor came out to open the batting. Both of them had been playing for the past three years, and were very good batsmen.

Jatin set the field and gave the ball to Jamshed. The contest had started.

Kishor started aggressively. As it was a limited over match, it was important to maintain a good run rate. Vidya Mandir started with an impressive run rate.

In the fifth over, Jamshed delivered a good ball, which Kishor could not play well. The ball remained in the air for some time, but fell considerably short of Amit who was fielding in the square leg position. Amit ran forward and picked up the ball and wicketkeeper Mahendra and other fielders clapped to appreciate Jamshed's delivery.

"Amit, stay in front," shouted Jatin, asking Amit to field in the short leg position. There was a good chance of a catch in this close fielding position.

The next ball from Jamshed was also on the leg side, but Kishor, who was anticipating such a delivery, was prepared for it. Going on his back foot, Kishor turned his bat in a power-packed stroke.

Amit saw the ball approach him like lightning. He tried to take an evasive action, but was too late. The ball hit the back of his head with full force. Amit stumbled to the ground.

There was chaos on the field. All players ran to Amit. Kishor, who was terrified, was the first to be there. Amit was unconscious, his head bleeding profusely.

"Take him to the tent," said Jatin, visibly upset. "The school doctor would have come."

Four players lifted Amit and walked towards the tent. When they reached half way to the tent, Amit regained consciousness. He walked the rest of the distance, supported by two players. Parimal had come to the front, and he took charge of Amit, as he reached the tent. He took Amit to the dispensary, where the doctor had just come. The doctor cleaned the wound, but suggested that they go to a hospital, since the bleeding was considerable. After some first aid, Parimal took Amit to the hospital.

The doctor in the hospital examined the wound carefully and said: "Fortunately, it is not very deep, and there is no internal injury, so there is no reason to worry. Only he has lost a lot of blood, so he would need to rest."

He applied fresh dressing on Amit's head. His head was now entirely covered by the bandage. Amit had started feeling better, although the pain was still severe, and he felt weak and giddy.

As they left the hospital, Parimal asked him: "Shall I take you home?"

"No," said Amit weakly. "Let's go back to school. I want to see the match."

"You won't be able to play," said Parimal.

"I know. But I still want to see the match. I will rest for a while in the dispensary, and then sit in our tent."

There was a cot in the dispensary. Amit lay down, and fell asleep shortly. When he awoke, Parimal was sitting in a chair next to him.

"How are you feeling now?" he asked.

"Better," said Amit. "I am still feeling a little weak though."

As soon as Amit got up, he felt faint, and Parimal had to hold him. "Will you be able to walk to the tent?" asked Parimal.

Amit steadied himself, and gingerly walked towards the tent. As soon as he entered the tent, and some of the people in the tent saw him with his bandaged head, there was a buzz in the tent. A lot of students came to him and asked him how he was. He walked along the aisle towards the players' chairs in the front.

The girls were sitting on the other side of the aisle. Amit saw that Varsha had turned around, and was looking at him. He had hoped that she would come to him, and inquire about his health. She stared at him for a long time, but then shifted her gaze.

The break between the innings was going on, and all players from Navjivan's team were back.

"How are you feeling?" Jatin asked him. "Are you going to be able to play?"

Amit showed him the bandage in response. "Doctor has advised him to rest," said Parimal.

"What has happened in the match so far?" Amit asked.

Jatin shook his head. "They have scored too many runs," he said. "When the forty overs were bowled, they had scored a hundred and seventy-eight for five wickets."

"We will have to score nearly four-and-a-half runs an over," said Amit. It sounded a little beyond their reach. But by way of encouragement, he said, "You can do it. You and Pravin should give a good start. Then you have Vikram."

"But now we don't have you," said Jatin. "I was counting on you."

Coming from Jatin, this sounded strange. Was there a sudden spurt of sympathy? Was that because Amit was so badly injured? Or was it because of the support that Amit had given to Jatin on Friday?

The break was over, and it was time for the second innings to start. The fielding side emerged from Vidya Mandir's tent. Jatin and Pravin were ready with their bats, and they also came out on the ground. Amit sat in his chair in the front row.

He learnt from Ghanshyam that his injury had shaken up Kishor, and he got out almost immediately after Amit had left the field. But the other batsmen had also played well. For a long time, Navjivan had been able to keep the run-rate under control, but the last few overs had yielded too many runs. Jagadish, with fifty-two was the highest scorer.

Jatin was a very good batsman, and he started with a four off the first ball. Everyone was excited in Navjivan's tent and started clapping and chanting Jatin's name. Amit forgot his injury, and got absorbed in the match.

The first seven overs yielded thirty-five runs, of which twenty were scored by Jatin. Pravin was also batting very sensibly. Everyone in Navjivan's tent was happy. If they played like this, crossing the score of a hundred and seventy-eight was not impossible.

But in the eighth over, Pravin missed a straight delivery from Manhar. The dreadful sound of the ball hitting the stumps dashed any hope that Pravin may have had of having survived. Angry with himself, he walked back to the tent, and Vikram came out to replace him.

As Amit was not going to bat, this was the last pair of good batsmen.

Vikram opened the scoring with an elegant stroke for three runs. Manhar ended a successful over, and Vikram held his strike.

The bowler from the other end was Pradeep. The third ball of his over whizzed past the off side. Vikram had attempted to cut, and the ball took an edge of the bat. There was uproar from the wicketkeeper and the close-in fielders, and Vikram turned around to see that wicketkeeper Mahesh had taken a very good catch and was jumping joyfully. Pradeep ran towards him and lifted him up.

Navjivan was depending heavily on Vikram but he came back after scoring only three runs. If Amit had not been hurt, he would have come in to bat at this juncture. But in his absence, it was Dilip, who came out of the tent. The time he took walking to the pitch was more than the time he stayed at the pitch, because on the very next ball that Pradeep bowled, he got out and returned back.

"What is happening?" said Pravin, aghast. "We are heading for a disgraceful defeat! It would be difficult to show our faces in the market tomorrow!"

Prakash, the next batsman, was not even ready yet. No one had imagined that wickets would tumble so fast. As no one emerged from the tent for some time, someone shouted from the opposite tent, "What happened? Are you giving up?"

Prakash was so dazed when he came out that Jatin met him half way and gave him a few hints. Prakash batted out the rest of the over without lifting his bat.

At the end of nine overs, the score was thirty-eight for three. The scoring rate was falling behind, but Jatin's priority at this time was to steady the innings.

Prakash followed Jatin's advice, and batted without taking any chances. Neither batsman attempted any flamboyant strokes, and took singles whenever they could. When twenty overs were bowled, Navjivan had scored sixty-seven for three. Jatin was thirty-seven and Prakash ten.

At the end of twenty overs, the players went to their tents for water and soft drinks.

"The two of you have done well to keep your wickets intact," Pravin said. "But now we need some quick runs."

"I plan to hit out now," said Jatin. "And I want Prakash to keep one end up."

But that tactic did not work. The drinks interval had broken Prakash's concentration, and in the first over after the break, he got out. Jitendra went two balls later, in the same over; and Navjivan were in trouble once again.

"We don't have any batsmen left," said Pravin to Amit. "I wish Jatin had listened to me, and kept those four in our side."

Ghanshyam was the next batsman in. He wasn't particularly adept at the batting techniques, but riding on his luck, he hit three consecutive boundaries. There was a wave of excitement in Navjivan's tent once more, and everyone stood up and cheered.

But Ghanshyam's luck did not last very long. When Navjivan's score was eighty-seven, he got out.

Navjivan's wicketkeeper Mahendra gave Jatin company for about four overs. In the twenty-eighth over, first Mahendra, and then Jamshed returned back. The score then was ninety-eight, and eight wickets had fallen. Ravi, who was the last player, barring Amit, came out to bat.

That the match could now get over any moment was a depressing thought for everyone in Navjivan tent. There was no chance of a victory: the only interest left was the margin of defeat.

"It is going to be the most humiliating defeat in the last three years," said Pravin mournfully. "Jatin is playing well, but no one has given him any support."

"We have been hounded by bad luck," Vikram said. "We lost four of our best batsmen, and then Amit got hurt."

"I had told Jatin that our batting would be extremely weakened," reminded Pravin. "And it got further weakened because Amit could not play."

There was depressed silence for a minute. Amit broke that. "I think I will go out to play," he said unexpectedly.

Everyone looked at him. "How are you going to play?" asked Ghanshyam. "Hasn't the doctor asked you to rest?"

"I have rested enough," said Amit. "And I am feeling much better now." His head was still throbbing, but the weakness was gone. "I don't know how much I would be able to help. But if I can give some support to Jatin, the margin of defeat may be more respectable."

Just then, Jatin hit a four, and Navjivan crossed a hundred.

"We still have a very long way to go, Amit," Vikram said. "Do you think your taking this risk will help?"

"Whatever I can contribute will be a help," said Amit. "Give me the pads and gloves."

On the first ball of the thirtieth over, Ravi got out. Navjivan's score at that time was a hundred and five. With the fall of Ravi's wicket, the players of Vidya Mandir embraced and congratulated each other. Jatin started walking back with Ravi, his head down.

Suddenly, there was a sound of applause from Navjivan's tent, and Amit, with his head covered in a bandage, and Pravin to run for him emerged.

Jatin was taken aback when he saw Amit come out. "Amit, are you going to bat?"

"I will try," said Amit.

Happy that the defeat had been postponed, Jatin walked back to the pitch. "Take a single early," he told Amit. "I will try and keep the strike after that."

Amit stood at the batting crease and looked around. Both tents were full. He saw his friends in Navjivan's tent. They must be expecting me to last long, and score, thought Amit. Varsha must also be sitting in the tent, watching Amit. He was quite used to playing big matches with spectators watching. But Amit wished that he were playing his first big match for Navjivan under better circumstances.

Girish continued to bowl his unfinished over. Amit played the first ball defensively. The next ball, he turned towards fine leg. Jatin and Pravin crossed for a single. The ball had travelled far, and a second run was possible. It was Amit's call whether he would be able to bat, or he wanted Jatin to keep the strike.

"Second," he shouted, and Jatin and Pravin crossed over again.

Amit was happy that he had opened the scoring. The spectators also applauded Amit.

Amit faced the next ball with more confidence. Stepping out of the crease, he hit the ball straight. The ball went past Girish so fast, that Girish found it safer to move away from the line of the ball. The ball travelled beyond the boundary for four runs.

Jatin raised his bat, and thumped it to appreciate the stroke. There was a roar in Navjivan's tent. Amit suppressed a smile of happiness, and got ready to face the next ball with confidence.

Amit cut the last ball of the over, and got a single. That gave Amit the strike in the next over also.

Gradually, Amit grew in confidence. The sense of timing and movement of feet improved. Amit had always found an inexplicable strength in him whenever he stood at the pitch with the bat in his hand. He forgot his injury completely.

Both he and Jatin played sensibly. They did not take undue risks, but took full advantage of loose deliveries and kept pushing the score slowly but surely. Jatin completed his fifty, and the team score reached a hundred and thirty-five in the thirty-fifth over. Even if they lost at this stage, the defeat would be far less disgraceful. But for the first time, the three players assessed the prospect of winning. They required about nine runs per over from that point. It was difficult, and the required rate was likely to keep climbing.

In the penultimate over, Amit took a single, to bring up a hundred and fifty. Then Jatin hit two consecutive boundaries. Excitement was mounting among the spectators. The three players conferred and decided that Jatin would take a single off the last ball, and keep the strike in the final over. Jatin hit the last ball, and they ran a single; but saw that the fielder chasing the ball had slipped and fallen down. The ball had rolled across the boundary line. The team score had reached a hundred and sixty-two, but the strike was now with Amit.

The atmosphere in Navjivan's tent was charged with excitement. There was a complete transformation from the air of diffidence and despondency that had prevailed there not much long ago.

There was another mid-wicket conference among the three Navjivan players before the final over of the innings started. "Sixteen to equal, seventeen to win," said Jatin. "Hit out. And if you can't, take a single and give the strike to me."

Pradeep was going to deliver the final over. Each bowler got a maximum of eight overs, and the last over was reserved for Vidya Mandir's fastest and most successful bowler.

Amit hit the first ball very powerfully. But it went straight to Manhar, who fielded it deftly. Amit could not even take a single. He banged his bat on the ground impatiently, and Pravin ran up to him, asking him to calm down.

The second ball was a short-pitched bouncer. Amit went on his back foot, covered the wickets and hooked. With one bounce, the ball crossed the boundary line.

Everyone was on their feet in Navjivan's tent. Amid thunderous clapping, Amit could hear his name being cheered. Trying to preserve his concentration, Amit got ready to face the third ball.

The third ball was pulled towards mid-wicket. Two fielders ran after the ball, but could not stop it.

Jatin had come up to Amit in order to take a run. He patted Amit's shoulder, and went back to his place. Navjivan's score had raced to a hundred and seventy, and they now needed nine runs to win in three balls.

The fourth ball was pitched on the off stump. Amit went on his back foot and executed a square drive. The ball went like a bullet, bisected two fielders and reached the boundary line. A firecracker burst in Navjivan's tent. Amit saw students jumping and cheering. Would Varsha be cheering too? Amit thought.

Now Navjivan needed five runs for the victory. The next ball was going to be crucial. A four would equal the scores. Even a single would keep the victory within reach.

The fifth ball was another short-pitched ball. Once again, Amit tried to hook. There was a roar from the Navjivan camp. But this time, Amit had missed the ball completely, and Mahesh stopped the ball behind the stumps.

After a long time, there were cheers from Vidya Mandir's tent. They had seen a certain victory slipping away from their grasp. With this ball, their hopes of winning became strong once again.

Last ball. Jagadish, the captain of Vidya Mandir, assessed the field placement and made finer adjustments to it. Amit took his stance, leaning on the bat. Pradeep started the run up. The moment the ball left his hand, Amit sprang forward about three or four steps, and as soon as the ball hit the ground, he took it in the middle of the bat. Using all the power that he could find in his shoulders and arms, he turned the bat. The ball went over Pradeep's head, and kept going up and up, and finally disappeared in the trees behind Navjivan's tent.

The umpire raised his hands to signal a six, but that was a mere formality. The moment the ball passed over Pradeep's head, Navjivan's victory was certain. Jatin leaped towards Amit, grabbed him in his arms and hugged him. Pravin joined them and embraced both of them together. Jagadish shook hands with Jatin and Amit, and all players from Vidya Mandir clapped to applaud the heroic feat performed by this last pair.

The scenes in Navjivan's tent were unbelievable. Pandemonium had broken out and all players and other students were dancing. Most students had rushed to the front to welcome their heroes. Crackers had been set off behind the tent.

Jatin was feeling on top of the world. After two years, Navjivan had regained its lost reputation. It was a dream come true for him. He was also the highest scorer in the match with seventy runs. Amit had scored fifty-two.

As Jatin and Amit reached the tent, all boys lifted them up, and amid cheers, brought them in. Amit started feeling dizzy again, and the boys released him. He looked at the back of the tent. Varsha was standing with Trupti.

The thought that kept coming to him over and over was: Varsha had seen his heroic display. She was present throughout, and must have clapped, shouted and cheered as her school raced towards an impossible victory. Surely, she will forget the misunderstanding that had been created earlier, and congratulate him today. She may not come to the front, because the boys were still creating a ruckus there. He would have to go to the back of the tent.

Arrangement for drinking water was in the rear. Amit was thirsty, and that gave him a good reason to go to the rear of the tent. On the way, Purnima and two girls from the Eighth saw him. They all waved their congratulations at him. Amit waved back, but he did not pause to talk to them.

The girls had started to walk out of the tent in a file that was passing by the water fountain. Amit reached the water fountain. Varsha would pass by him in a few moments.

When Amit was drinking water, Varsha and Trupti passed by. Trupti was closer to Amit, but she was talking to Varsha with her face turned, and could not see Amit. Varsha could. Amit heard Varsha speak.

"I wish we had gone to a cinema," she was saying. "I find cricket matches so boring!"

❖

CHAPTER 9

Annual Day

The school reopened on the second January after the winter break. The injury to Amit's head had completely healed by then, and his bandage had been removed. As he entered the school, many students asked him how he was. Jatin was among the first to inquire.

Amit could see from the first day that Jatin's attitude towards him had changed completely. Earlier, he used to maintain a distance with Amit, and treat him with skepticism. After the cricket match, he had developed genuine respect for Amit and seemed eager to treat him as a friend.

Tuesday fell on the third, and the Student Council met on that day. Amit noted the presence of Sushilaben and Dineshbhai at this meeting, which surprised him, as he had never seen them in the Student Council meetings.

Bhanubhai expressed his happiness at the outcome of the cricket match and conveyed his congratulations to the captain and the entire team. "Two major events will take place before we meet next month," he went on. "The Annual Day of the school and the Funfair."

The faces of those present at the meeting shone with delight. Both these were events that everyone looked forward to.

"First the Annual Day," said Bhanubhai, warming to the subject. "This year we are going to hold it on the Republic Day, on the twenty-sixth. We will have flag hoisting in the morning, as usual. In the evening, we will have a cultural programme in the open-air theatre in the back of the school building."

Amit had seen the huge open space behind the building, next to the hobby classes and the canteen. There was a stage connected to the building, facing an open space where a large audience could be accommodated.

"Every year, the cultural programme that we perform is regarded as the best among such programmes performed by schools in Baroda, and I expect that the same standard will be maintained this year also. Many parents come to see the programme by invitation, and some of them buy tickets to bring their guests. The programme is a symbol of prestige for this school, and all efforts must be made to make it a grand success."

Bhanubhai was saying this so seriously, that it left no doubt in Amit's mind that this was a very important occasion for the school. Suddenly the Principal turned to him and asked, "Amit, if I remember correctly, you are in charge of cultural activities. Am I right?"

"Yes sir," said Amit.

"In that case, you will have to play a very important role. The success of the entire programme may depend on you. I suggest that you identify a few students to help you with different aspects of the arrangement. They don't have to be from this Council. Sushilaben, Dineshbhai and Nirmalaben will also play a role in the arrangement. So you should discuss with them later and find out what they want from you."

"I will do that, sir," said Amit, casting a glance at Sushilaben and Dineshbhai. He would enjoy working with them.

"The programme will have entries like dances, *garba, ras*, chorus songs and skits. The last item, as always, will be a play. The play is always the most important item, because it leaves the strongest impression on the audience. Sushilaben has selected a play, and Amit, I think you should go through the script, because I want you to also help in selecting the cast."

Amit took note of that, happy at the important role that he would have to play in the Annual Day function.

"Rehearsals will be conducted by Sushilaben and Dineshbhai. For all those who are not aware of the multi-talented personality of Dineshbhai, he is not only excellent in arts and crafts; he is equally talented in dramatics. We place a lot of emphasis on costumes and the set for the play. Costumes are hired from outside, but the set is always made by the students in the hobby classes, under the supervision of Dineshbhai."

Evidently Dineshbhai was going to play a key role in this programme, Amit thought.

"Nirmalaben, (who was the music teacher in the school), will take the responsibility for all music and dance programmes," Bhanubhai continued. "Each class will have one item to perform, and obviously all class teachers will have to assume responsibility for the items of their respective classes."

The Principal turned to Amit once again. "Your role, along with the other students you nominate to help you, will be crucial on the day of the programme. The entire organization will have to be provided by you. Making the open-air theatre ready, receiving the parents and seating them, selling tickets to guests, preparing the stage and everything that goes on behind the stage would be your responsibility," he said. "Amit, when you had decided to take charge of cultural activities in the beginning of the year, had you realized what will be required of you? And now that you know what is involved, do you feel confident of being able to carry out your responsibilities? If you have any doubt, this is the time to say so. Because once you have taken the responsibility, I would like to see that it is carried out successfully."

Amit once again stole a glance at the two teachers, and saw encouragement in their eyes. "I am confident, sir," he said. "I will speak to the teachers today and start the preparations immediately."

He knew that Parimal, Ketan, Ghanshyam and others would be very happy to help him. Even Purnima and other girls would be willing to help. Everyone except Varsha.

The discussion about the Annual Day was over for that day. "Now for the funfair," said the Principal. "On Saturday, the fourth of February, we will have funfair in the playground. Each class will get two, or at the most, three stalls. They may organize games or sell food items that they have prepared. The Class Representatives will decide with the class teachers how many stalls the class should have, who will manage them and what they will have in them. The Class Representatives themselves need not manage the stalls. In fact, they should not, because the Representatives of the Eighth and Ninth standards will be required to help in organizing the funfair. We are giving the task of erection and decoration of stalls to an outside contractor, and the senior Class Representatives must supervise that activity."

That afternoon, Amit met Sushilaben and asked her for the script of the play. She did not have the script with her at that time, but promised to give it the next day. Amit met Dineshbhai and Nirmalaben also. From the music teacher, he learnt that the girls from the Ninth standard were going to sing a chorus song. Varsha was going to take a leading role in the chorus, and was also going to sing one stanza herself.

The next day, Sushilaben gave him the script, and Amit went through it at night. The play appeared to be a very good one, and he felt that if it were acted well, the audience would thoroughly enjoy it. Besides the hero and the heroine, it had six more characters.

When the science period was going on the next day, a peon came to call Amit. "Principal wants you," he said.

When Amit entered Bhanubhai's office, he saw that Sushilaben and Dineshbhai were also present.

"Come in, Amit," said Bhanubhai. "Did you read the script? How did you find it?"

"It is a very good script, sir," said Amit. "If it is acted well, everyone will enjoy it."

"Good acting alone may not be enough. The play is such that we will need very good sets also, right Dineshbhai?"

Dineshbhai nodded. "The entire action is in a very rich family's home," he said. "If we do not have proper sets to give that effect, the play will look a bit bland."

"And are we capable of making the necessary sets?" asked Bhanubhai.

"Yes," said Dineshbhai. "We have some thick hardboard from last year. We will have to buy the rest. I am starting the activity in my classes today. By the twenty-sixth, the sets will be ready."

"Good. As you said, sets will play a crucial role in making the play effective. Do you need any help from Amit or his team?"

"Not in preparing the sets," said Dineshbhai. "But I will need help in erecting them. The play is the last item in that programme, and there is an interval before the play. We will have to erect the set during that interval. It is something that can be done with the help of about four or five boys."

"Okay, that settles the sets," said Bhanubhai. "Now the cast. Sushilaben, any suggestions?"

Sushilaben turned to Amit. "Amit, would you like to take the lead role?"

This was unexpected and Amit had not thought about it. He was not very keen to act on the stage. He remembered the elocution competition. Although he was certain that such fiasco would not happen again, he said: "I would like to, but I think I will be so tied up with the organization, that I will not be able to take any roles."

Everyone agreed with him, and finally it was decided that the role of the hero would go to a boy from the Eighth standard.

"Varsha had borrowed the script from me a few days back," said Sushilaben. "She came back and expressed her interest in the role of the heroine. I think she would be ideal for that role."

"Varsha again?" thought Amit. "No wonder she is so arrogant. Why can't anyone think of any other girl in the school?" Aloud he said: "I think we ought to give that role to someone else."

He must have said this quite vehemently, because everyone present turned to him in surprise. "Why do you say this?" asked Sushilaben.

"Firstly, the hero is from the Eighth standard. It would look odd if the heroine is from a higher class," said Amit. "Second, Varsha is taking a leading part in the chorus. It is not as if she would be left out of the programme if she does not get this role. Third, everyone in our school knows Varsha. She sings the invocations in the morning assembly; she takes part in other activities as well. Why not give chance to some other girl who hasn't had an opportunity to show her talent?"

"And fourth," said Amit in his mind, "it is time she left her high horses and came down to earth."

"What Amit is saying makes sense," said Bhanubhai. "We know that Varsha would act the role of the heroine very well. But we should give opportunity to others also. Do you have anyone else in mind?"

"Some months back Bhairavi had met me," said Amit. "She is in the Eighth, and has joined the school this year. She is interested in dramatics and has experience also. Being new in this school, she hasn't had a chance to show her talent. I am quite sure that given a chance, she will do very well."

Bhanubhai looked at Sushilaben. "You haven't made any promises to Varsha, have you?"

"No, I haven't given her any decision. But she will get very disappointed if she does not get the role she was looking forward to."

"Explain to her that it is not that we don't have confidence in her. In fact, we know she would play that role very well. Our intention is only to develop other talent also."

"Perhaps we can offer her a smaller role in the play," suggested Dineshbhai. "There are other characters too, besides the heroine."

"That's not a bad suggestion," said Bhanubhai. "Also, speak to Bhairavi and assess how good she would be for the role of the heroine. Now, let us start the preparation for the play immediately."

Amit was happy with the decisions taken. Varsha had been behaving very strangely with him in the last few weeks. The sting of her behaviour after the cricket match was still fresh in his mind. It was necessary to teach her a lesson.

He was sure that Varsha would know that Amit had a part to play in this decision. She was present when Bhanubhai had told Amit that he would help in selecting the cast. She had seen the peon call him to the Principal's office in the morning.

Sushilaben must have broken the news to Varsha during the lunch break, because immediately after the break, she appeared very different. Disappointment and anger showed on her face. The look that she gave Amit told him without doubt that she held Amit responsible for the decision. Sushilaben told Amit in the afternoon that Bhairavi had been offered the role of the heroine. She also said that Varsha had declined the smaller role, which was offered to her.

By now, Amit knew Varsha very well. He was sure that Varsha would boycott the whole programme. He soon found out that he was right. He learnt from Purnima a few days later, that Varsha had withdrawn from the chorus and the lines that she was going to sing had been given to Trupti. Amit could not find out what excuse Varsha had given for withdrawing from the chorus. It must have been a very convincing excuse, because neither Sushilaben nor Bhanubhai suspected that she had done this out of protest against being denied the heroine's role. Amit had expected that Varsha would not even come to see the programme. But one day, Bhanubhai announced in the assembly that attendance at that programme was compulsory, particularly for the Class Representatives. So Varsha would not be able to wiggle out of seeing the programme.

The rehearsals for the play had started. Amit used to go and see the rehearsal everyday after cricket. Everyone was rehearsing earnestly. Bhairavi was standing out in her role.

Amit felt very happy for having suggested Bhairavi's name for the heroine's role. She was an extremely warm and modest girl. She had expressed genuine gratitude to Amit for giving her the opportunity. Would Varsha have done that? Each time that Amit saw Bhairavi, he unconsciously compared her with Varsha. Bhairavi was a very cheerful and frank girl, without even a hint of arrogance. Her eyes would light up every time she smiled her infectious smile. In the beginning, Amit felt that her uneven teeth were a blemish; but later, he realized that it was those teeth that made her look more attractive. But he had to accept that Varsha was far prettier.

Varsha had become a very different person. Even in the class, she was quiet, withdrawn, gloomy and brooding. She no longer tried to be the centre of attention among girls, and remained aloof in the class. She ignored Amit completely, and did not even look at him. Amit often remembered the time when she had congratulated him after the election, and when she had sat with him and talked during the engagement function; and wondered where that warm and friendly girl had disappeared.

Parimal who attended the craft classes kept briefing him on the progress with the sets. Amit would also go to the craft class frequently, and Dineshbhai would show him the sets under preparation with a lot of interest. The sets were coming up very well, and would brighten up the stage when they were erected. Bhanubhai kept checking with Amit about the progress of the rehearsals and the sets, and sometimes visited the craft room and expressed his satisfaction. As the twenty-sixth drew closer, the intensity of work increased. The craft class would work beyond five thirty, and after all students left, Dineshbhai would apply finishing touches to the work done on that day.

Amit stayed in school till very late in the evening on the twenty-fifth. All activities – music, dance, crafts and dramatics – were in full swing. Amit had asked Ghanshyam to bring the costumes. He came back with the dresses for the dances, *garba, ras* and the play. With help from the teachers, Amit made sure that the dresses were in good condition, and kept them in a huge wardrobe in Dineshbhai's room. The sets were nearly complete. Dineshbhai was going to apply a final touch tomorrow. The people for decorating the theatre area were coming tomorrow, and Amit made sure by reminding them that they came on time.

Amit couldn't sleep that night. He kept thinking about the programme. Everything was going so well, that there seemed to be no reason to worry, but until the last item was over, Amit was going to feel tense. The programme was very important for his school, and Bhanubhai had made him responsible.

The next day started with flag hoisting in front of the school building. Bhanubhai performed the usual ceremony and gave a brief speech. All twelve Class Representatives were standing with him, near the flag. Amit and Varsha had to stand side by side, but neither of them looked at the other.

Immediately after the flag hoisting, Amit went through the building to the rear side. Dineshbhai was also with him. Both went to the craft class.

The classroom was in a mess today. Pieces of hardboard, cardboard and paper were strewn around everywhere. Paint marks were seen all over the floor.

"The whole of tomorrow, we will be cleaning up this mess," Dineshbhai said with a smile, and started on his work.

Amit saw that paper was stuck on the hardboard and cardboard, and was painted with water paint. Windows, the view of the outside world as seen from the windows, doors and all were painted painstakingly on those boards. When erected on the stage, they would create the aura of the drawing room in a rich house.

At the moment, though, the boards were lying on the floor. The entire room was filled with them. The benches and easels used by the students were all stacked in a corner of the room. On one side of the room was Dineshbhai's table and opposite that was the huge cupboard.

Just as Dineshbhai finished his work, Bhanubhai entered the room. He inspected the sets closely, and said, "Very good. Dineshbhai and his students have done an excellent job. Now Amit, these sets are your responsibility."

"Keep them here for now," said Dineshbhai. "Things would be so chaotic near the stage that if we take the sets there, they may get spoiled. The stage is not very far. During the interval, we will shift the set to the stage and erect it. Keep a few volunteers ready."

Amit had already asked Parimal, Ketan, Ghanshyam and three more boys to help with the sets. Purnima had volunteered to receive the guests and take them to their seats. Three girls from smaller classes were going to help her. Parimal had also agreed to be at the reception counter to sell tickets and account for the money received.

Presently a truck arrived carrying chairs, which got placed in the theatre. Three sides of the theatre were cordoned off so that the entry to the theatre was restricted. At the entrance, a table was placed from where Parimal was going to sell tickets to the guests. A curtain was installed on the stage, lights were placed, loud speakers were mounted, and the entire place started humming with activity. Amit was at the centre of these activities, assisted by a troop of volunteers, and supervised by Dineshbhai.

This commotion lasted the entire afternoon. At about four, the girls taking part in dances and *garbas* started to get dressed. Dineshbhai gave them their dresses from the cupboard in his room, and the girls went to different classrooms to wear them. There was so much activity behind the stage that Amit did not get a moment of rest. From time to time, he peeped into the craft room to keep an eye on the sets.

Amit's parents were coming to see the show, but he had told them that he would be so tied up that he would not be able to meet them. Even after the show was over, they were going back on their own. Amit would have to settle a few things before he could leave.

At six, the parents started to arrive. By six-thirty, the theatre was full, and more people were still coming in. Exactly at six-thirty, the curtain was raised. A student from the Eighth had taken the role of the compere. He welcomed everyone and with an invocation by girls from the Fifth, the show got under way.

Amit was continually running around behind the stage, ensuring that everything required for the next item was at hand, all participants were available when they were required on the stage, and so on. He rarely got a chance to see how the show was proceeding. But he kept an eye on the audience and saw that they were all thoroughly enjoying the show and applauding every item. He located Varsha in the audience. She was sitting sullenly in the back row, away from her usual company, and watching the programme without interest.

Amit was interested in the chorus to be sung by the girls of his class, so as soon as the chorus started, he came out in the theatre area. He had never been to the rehearsal of this item, and was seeing it for the first time. He was quite impressed with the way everyone was singing in the chorus. Trupti sang her solo lines well, and there was a spontaneous applause, even in the middle of the song, when she finished her lines. But Amit had to admit that Varsha was a far better singer.

There was an item by the Tenth standard immediately after the chorus. After that a *ras*, and then the interval.

The play was to start immediately after the interval. Amit had decided that as soon as the *ras* started, he would go backstage and arrange to shift the set.

Amit was feeling quite tired after the hectic day. He found an empty chair, and sat there. Once the play started, the tension on his mind would begin to ease. The programme so far had been very good, and he was quite sure that the play would be like icing on the cake.

Purnima was standing not far from him. She saw Amit and came close to him. "It has been a wonderful programme," she said. "Bhanubhai would be very pleased." Amit felt very grateful for the support that he had received from everyone, and decided that over the next few days he would personally thank all those who had worked with him.

He got up as soon as the *ras* began, and went behind the stage. The commotion behind the stage had subsided, since all those who had finished their items had been asked to come out in the theatre area, and sit with other students. So only those who were connected with the play were behind the stage. Bhairavi was ready, clad in a *sari*. She blushed when she saw Amit, and flashed a smile, her eyes twinkling.

"Nervous?" asked Amit.

Bhairavi shook her head in confidence.

"Do well," Amit said, and walked on.

As he reached the craft class, he heard footsteps of someone running towards him. It was Parimal. He was carrying an envelope in his hands.

"I don't think any more guests will come now," he said. "In any case, there are no vacant seats left. So I am closing the sale of tickets."

"Okay," said Amit. "What's in your hand?"

"The gate money collected from the sale of tickets," said Parimal. "I wanted to give that to you." Parimal gave the envelope to Amit. "Exactly seven hundred and fifty rupees."

"Have you counted?" asked Amit. He did not have the time to count.

"Yes," said Parimal.

"Okay," said Amit. "I will locate Manibhai later in the evening and give it to him. In the meantime, will you call Ghanshyam and the other volunteers? We have to start shifting the sets."

Parimal disappeared, and Amit entered the craft class. He wanted to make sure one last time that the sets were all right.

It was about seven-thirty, and quite dark outside. The room was dimly lit by a solitary lamp. Amit cast a quick glance at the sets. All boards were where they were lying earlier, and nothing seemed to have been shifted. And yet, Amit felt that there was something strange. He looked at the sets more carefully.

And then he realized what had happened.

There was water all over the boards. Watercolour had started to dissolve. In some places, it had been completely wiped out.

At first Amit could not believe his eyes. Then he was so bewildered that he placed the envelope that he was carrying on Dineshbhai's table and rushed forward. He bent down and touched the sets. He realized that the board had become moist and soft, colours had run and the sets were not in usable condition at all.

A bucket of water lay close to the sets, turned on one side. Amit had seen this bucket earlier, and fearing that someone might trip over it, he had placed it aside. But evidently, that was just what had happened. He was very angry with himself that he did not empty it before placing it aside. His carelessness had resulted in unimaginable damage.

The first thought that came to Amit was to go and inform Dineshbhai. He ran out of the room. He could not see Dineshbhai anywhere behind the stage. He looked out, but he could not find him with the audience either. He came back to the craft room, and met Himanshu near the class.

"Do you know where Dineshbhai is?" asked Amit with desperation in his voice.

"When I saw him last, he was going towards the music class," said Himanshu.

Amit ran towards the music class. Just then, Dineshbhai emerged from that room. "Amit, I am glad you are here," he said. "The interval will start soon. Let us organize to shift the sets."

"Dineshbhai," started Amit. He did not know how he was going to break the news. "There has been an awful accident. Water has been spilled over the sets."

"What?" asked Dineshbhai with a start, and ran towards his class. Amit followed him.

Dineshbhai uttered exclamations of dismay as soon as he saw the sets. "These are completely useless now," he said. He noticed the bucket and asked, "Did you trip over it?"

"No," said Amit. "I have been coming here every now and then. This accident must have occurred only about fifteen minutes back. I have no idea by whom."

Dineshbhai went closer to the sets and bent down to examine them. Amit remembered that Dineshbhai had worked on the sets untiringly for weeks and had given the finishing touches to the sets only that morning. Now his efforts, and the efforts of the entire class had literally been washed away. He felt sorry for him and all those in his class.

But more than that, he was extremely worried about Bhanubhai's reaction. For Bhanubhai, this programme was a prestige symbol and the play the most important part of the programme. He had stressed the need for good sets throughout, and had been keeping a watch on the progress of the sets personally. Only this morning, he had asked Amit to assume the responsibility for the sets, and now this had happened.

Dineshbhai completed his examination. He looked at Amit and shook his head sadly. "These sets have become useless," he said.

"What are we going to do?" said Amit.

"Since we cannot use these sets, and will not be able to produce new ones in the next fifteen minutes, the answer is obvious," said Dineshbhai. "We will have to stage the play without sets."

"But how will we inform Bhanubhai?" asked Amit nervously.

Dineshbhai saw the expression on Amit's face and smiled. "Leave that to me," he said, patting Amit on his shoulder. "He would be surrounded by parents now. But I will call him aside and tell him what has happened." He left the room.

Dineshbhai had always been Amit's favourite teacher. Now Amit's admiration for him scaled new heights. His attitude had been very comforting, and Amit's worries lessened slightly.

As Amit was getting out of the room, he remembered the envelope containing the gate money that Parimal had given him. He turned towards Dineshbhai's table to pick it up, and got another nasty shock. There was no envelope on the table.

He was sure that he had left the envelope on that table when he had first seen that there was water on the sets. After that he had left the room for only five minutes, when he had gone to look for Dineshbhai. He had forgotten to take the envelope with him at that time. Where could it have disappeared in that period?

He frantically searched in the drawers and under the table. He started feeling dizzy. What was happening suddenly?

Amit decided to check with everyone behind the stage. As he ran towards the stage, he saw Parimal and Ghanshyam come towards him.

"What happened, Amit?" asked Parimal. "Why are you looking so haggard?"

Amit told them about the sets first.

"Really?" asked Parimal. He had also worked on the sets. "Are they completely useless?"

Then Amit told them about the misplaced envelope.

"Amit, you are in deep trouble," said Ghanshyam, worried. Amit had never seen him so serious. "What will Bhanubhai say?"

"That's what worries me," said Amit. The three of them inquired with everyone behind the stage whether anyone had been to the craft class recently, but nobody had.

The interval was going on. Amit saw Bhanubhai and Dineshbhai scurry towards the craft room. Silently, he followed them. When he reached the craft room, Bhanubhai was examining the sets.

"Where is Amit?" he thundered.

Amit came forward, visibly shaken.

"How did this happen?" demanded Bhanubhai angrily.

"I really don't know," said Amit feebly. "Only about fifteen minutes back, I had been to this room, and everything seemed to be all right."

"Who had access to this room?" asked Bhanubhai.

"Only Amit and I were required to come to this room," said Dineshbhai. "No one else had reason to be here."

"But somebody *did* come in and caused this havoc," said Bhanubhai. "Amit, you knew how important these sets were. I had made you responsible for them. Why did you leave the door open?"

"There were many other things required for tonight's programme in this room," said Amit. "Dineshbhai and I had to keep coming to the room frequently. But who else came in during the last fifteen minutes, I don't know."

"Find out," ordered Bhanubhai. "I want to know who is responsible for this damage."

Bhanubhai turned to leave the room. Amit's throat was dry. With great difficulty, he spoke. "Sir, there is something else that I have to tell you. I have misplaced some money."

"What money?" asked Bhanubhai.

"The money collected from the sale of tickets," said Amit. "It was in an envelope, and I had kept it on this table. When I went out to call Dineshbhai, I forgot to take the envelope with me. It was not there when I came back."

Amit had never seen a volcano erupt. Today he experienced it.

"Are you trying to tell me that you have misplaced the money that we collected by selling the tickets?" asked the Principal, sounding menacing. "That you were careless enough to leave that money lying around here when you left the room?"

"Only for five minutes," pleaded Amit. "I was so bewildered when I saw the condition of the sets that it did not occur to me to pick up the envelope from the table before leaving the room."

"Amit, I had considered you to be a very responsible boy," said Bhanubhai. "That is why I had placed all the responsibility for this programme on your shoulders. I had no idea that you were so careless. I will speak to you tomorrow. Parents are waiting for me now. But search the room thoroughly. You must have kept the envelope somewhere around and you don't remember."

He stormed out of the room, Dineshbhai behind him. Amit was left alone in the room. He did not know what to do. Following the Principal's instruction, he searched the room, although he knew that the search would be futile. The interval was over and the drama had started, but Amit was in no mood to see the drama. All he wanted to do was to go to the farthest classroom, lock himself in and cry loudly.

Having completed the search, when Amit came near the stage, the play had advanced considerably. Amit climbed down and came to the theatre area, and sat in the last row. The play was looking bland without the sets.

If Amit had watched the drama with interest, he would have seen that all the artistes were acting out their roles extremely well. Bhairavi was outstanding in her role and had captured the hearts of the audience. Even Varsha would not have performed so well.

At eight forty-five, the curtain fell. The audience gave a standing ovation to all the artistes. The drama was a resounding success.

Nobody had known about the drama that had been enacted behind the stage.

———◈◈◈———

CHAPTER 10

The Peace Bell

Amit did not sleep that night also. The next morning not only Amit, but also his parents were worried. They were more worried about the misplaced money than about the damage to the sets.

"Tell Bhanubhai," said Father, "that if you don't find the money, we will make good that amount. Even for the sets, if there is a damage that we have to pay, we would be willing to pay."

"Why don't *you* meet Bhanubhai?" Mother suggested.

"Amit would be able to fend for himself," Father said. "After that, if necessary, I will meet him."

Amit's younger sister, Alka, did not understand the gravity of the situation. She came to the dining table hopping, as usual, and gulped her milk.

"Amit," she said, as she passed her tongue over her creamy lips. "Yesterday I purchased a book of snack coupons. But when I counted later, I found that there were only nine pages."

"The person who prints these coupons makes mistakes sometimes," said Amit without interest. "Give me the book. I will change it for you."

"But I have used one coupon yesterday," said Alka.

"Never mind. We will tear off one coupon from the new book that we give you," said Amit, taking the book from Alka and putting it in his pocket.

That day, the topic of conversation everywhere in the school was the Annual Day programme. Everybody and their parents had loved the programme. Many students knew about the damage to the sets, but no one, except Parimal and Ghanshyam, knew about the loss of money.

Everybody saw that Amit was extremely depressed. Even during the assembly, he looked very grim. But even more serious was Bhanubhai. After the invocation, instead of his usual chatty speech, he merely said, "all Class Representatives will stay back", and adjourned the assembly.

Everyone filed out. Only twelve students and Bhanubhai remained in the hall. The twelve students stood in a semi-circle, and Bhanubhai perched himself on the corner of the table.

"All those who participated in yesterday's programme performed very well, and I would like to congratulate each one of them," said Bhanubhai. "But that is something that I will do in the assembly tomorrow. Before we start patting ourselves on our backs, let us look at some of our shortcomings.

"Two events took place yesterday, which have caused a great deal of anguish to me. For the last many days, the students of the craft class had been working on the sets for the play. Yesterday, somebody spilled water on the sets accidentally, and the sets became completely useless. Without these sets, the play was looking lifeless. We have done great injustice to the artistes who took part in that play, to the students and teachers who worked very hard to prepare the sets, and have hurt the prestige of this school. The sets were a responsibility of Amit at that time, and he is going to tell us how this came to happen."

Everyone looked at Amit. He was staring at the floor.

"But there was another incident, which was far more serious, and Amit is the person who will have to give an explanation for that episode also. Perhaps, most of you do not know about it. Amit, do you want to tell everyone what I am referring to?"

I wish Bhanubhai had not asked me to speak, thought Amit. He was not sure when his voice would break.

"Parimal gave me the money that he had collected from the sale of tickets," he said tonelessly. "When I saw the condition of the sets, I was so flabbergasted, that I left the envelope containing the money on Dineshbhai's table and ran out to call Dineshbhai. Five minutes later, when I came back, the envelope was missing." He looked at Bhanubhai and added, "That envelope contained seven hundred and fifty rupees. And I will pay this amount to the school."

"It is not a question of repaying the amount lost," shot back Bhanubhai. "It is the question of fulfilling your responsibilities. Today, as students, you have the responsibility for small amounts like this. Tomorrow, when you start your occupation, you may be responsible for amounts that are hundred times, thousand times more. You will not be able to repay, if you are careless with the money entrusted to you. In this school, we don't only learn languages and science;

we learn to be good and responsible citizens. And if the President of the Students' Council behaves so irresponsibly, it is a matter of shame for the school."

Amit's face was turning red. He did not look up.

"If you have misplaced the envelope, it has to turn up from somewhere," continued Bhanubhai. "Do you think you had placed the envelope somewhere else? Are you sure you did not take the envelope with you when you ran out of the classroom?"

Does Bhanubhai believe that I have taken the money and I am lying now? Amit thought. He said, "I am quite sure that I had kept it on Dineshbhai's table. In the five minutes that I was out of the room, someone must have entered the room and...."

"Amit," Bhanubhai stopped him. "Are you saying that someone from this school *stole* the money? Because if you are, it is a grave aspersion. And I will not accept it without proper evidence. Everyone in this school comes from good families. I cannot believe that anyone in our school would have the habit of stealing. If you resort to baseless allegations to cover up your carelessness, I will not accept it."

Amit did not know what to say. He kept quiet. He was conscious of everyone's gaze at him. He did not have the courage to look up.

"It was bad enough that the sets were damaged. But that was an accident. Money cannot be lost by accident. Extreme carelessness on the part of someone is responsible for it. Or as Amit would have me believe, someone's dishonesty. As the money was also in Amit's possession at that time, I want Amit to find out what happened to it. But remember, I will not accept baseless allegations against any student."

Bhanubhai paused for some time. Then he said, "Amit, I had lot of expectations from you, but yesterday, you have let me down very badly. If the President of the Students' Council cannot behave in a responsible manner, he provides a bad example for the other students. In past, I have never had to ask any President to step down from his position, but if I do not get satisfactory answers to both the questions before the next meeting of the Council, I will have to ask the Council to elect a new President."

Bhanubhai left the assembly hall abruptly. The other students also left the hall silently. Only Amit stood there, transfixed.

The next meeting of the Council was on the seventh of February – only ten days later. How he was going to get satisfactory answers to the two questions by that time, Amit had no idea. If he had to step down from the position of President, it would be most shameful. How would he ever show his face to anybody after that?

And worse, the position of President would most likely go to Varsha. That was even more unbearable. Varsha, his arch enemy, would be in the seventh heaven today. How she would have enjoyed seeing Amit being humiliated in front of everyone! Amit vaguely remembered that when Bhanubhai was talking, she was looking at him. By now, she would have told everyone in the class how he had been disgraced in front of the Council members. It was going to be difficult for him to go back to his class.

Amit remembered that the first period that day was Science, and everyone would have gone to the lab. He decided that he would not go to the lab today, but instead, stay in the classroom.

Varsha would be in the classroom, taking the notebooks before leaving for the lab. Amit waited for a few minutes, giving her time to leave the classroom. He did not want to face Varsha.

After spending a few idle moments in the assembly hall, Amit came out and went to his classroom. But he was surprised as he entered the class, for he found Varsha sitting in her seat. She did not appear to be going to the lab either. Amit changed his mind. He decided that he *would* go to the lab after all. Sitting in the classroom for half an hour with Varsha seemed unbearable to him.

As he opened his satchel and started to look for the science books, he realized that Varsha had got up from her seat and was walking towards him. Amit was very surprised. What could Varsha have in mind? Did she want to further humiliate him?

Amit kept his eyes in his satchel. Varsha came and stood next to him. After a while, she said, "Amit, I want to speak to you." It was the first time in six weeks that she had addressed him.

"What is it?" asked Amit, his gaze still in the satchel.

There was no response from Varsha for some time, so Amit looked up. He saw signs of hesitancy on her face. Finally she spoke.

"*I was the one who spilled water on the sets yesterday,*" she said. "*Deliberately.*"

Amit wasn't sure that he had heard correctly. "What?" he asked. The satchel had slipped from his hands.

Varsha sighed. "Yes, Amit," she said. "I was so mad at you that I did not realize what I was doing. Honest. When

I emptied the bucket, I felt extremely sorry. But by then, it was too late."

Amit's mind was in a whirl. "Did you decide to settle the score with me like this?" he asked incredulously. "By hurting the reputation of the school? By destroying everything that Dineshbhai and his students had worked so hard to create?"

"I thought of all that afterwards," said Varsha. "I was so angry with you, and the play, and the whole programme; that I did not know what I was doing. I had been hoping all the time that the play or the entire programme gets cancelled. Or you get into trouble and Bhanubhai scolds you. *Why did you keep me out of the play?*"

"I know you withdrew from the chorus as a mark of protest," said Amit. "And to be honest, I had expected that. But I thought that was the extent to which you would go."

"After I withdrew from the chorus, I found out that my lines had gone to Trupti," said Varsha with contempt. "What does she know about music?"

"She wasn't bad," said Amit.

"She *wasn't* bad?" echoed Varsha. "I thought you knew something about music. Can't you make out when somebody is completely tuneless?"

"Everybody seemed to have liked her lines," defended Amit.

"That is what angered me," said Varsha. "My withdrawing from the chorus did not serve any purpose."

"What do you mean it did not serve any purpose?" asked Amit with passion. "Did you think that you were *punishing* the school by withdrawing from the chorus? Did you expect that anyone who heard the song without your voice in it would *plead* to you to stay in the chorus? Did you expect that everyone in the school would do exactly what *you* wanted?"

"So far, everyone in this school *did* do everything I wanted," said Varsha. "At least everyone in our class. Till you came along. After that everything changed. For the picnic, I wanted to go to Vasad, but you took them to Pavagadh."

"*I* did not take anyone to Pavagadh, Varsha. It was decided democratically. But it is pointless to debate that now," said Amit. "And because we did not go where you had set your heart to go, you boycotted the picnic."

"I thought you would not enjoy the picnic. But all of you came back very happy. Amit, don't you have any idea what I was going through?" Suddenly, Varsha's eyes were filled with tears. "I was all alone in the class. With nobody I could share my feelings with. And then you kept me out of the play. Do you realize how I had felt?"

Varsha took a handkerchief and started to dab her eyes. Amit would have melted seeing her cry, but today he was very annoyed with Varsha.

"No matter how you felt, you had no right to spoil the sets," he said stiffly.

"I know what I did was wrong," said Varsha. "But I could not control myself. After hearing people applaud Trupti, I had lost my mind. I knew that if these people liked Trupti's singing, they would go crazy when they saw Bhairavi act. I decided that I wouldn't stay for the play. I got up immediately after the chorus.

"I did not want to leave from the front, because if Purnima or Parimal saw me, I would have to make an excuse for leaving early. So I quietly went backstage, and started walking towards the front of the building. On the way, I passed by the craft class, and there I saw the sets lying on the floor. I knew how important these sets were. I had heard Bhanubhai stress that, and give the responsibility for the sets to you. I saw no one in the room. A bucket filled with water was lying there.

"All the frustration and anger that was pent-up in me got released. I did not know what I was doing. When I saw the watercolour dissolve, I felt very sorry; but by then the deed was done, and I could not undo it."

Amit was trying hard to control his anger. A selfish, insolent and conceited girl was describing her crime, for which *he* was being punished.

"Just at that moment, I heard some voices outside. You were talking to Parimal. I got panicky. I could not imagine what would happen to me if you came in and saw me near the drenched sets. There was no time to leave the room. So I decided to hide inside the room. There is a large cupboard in the room. I hid behind the cupboard. From where I was hiding, I could see the door and the sets, which were to the left of the door, but I could not see the table on the right of the door.

"Then you entered," said Vasha. Yesterday's events were passing through her mind like a motion picture, and she spoke as if she was describing the pictures frame by frame. "You saw the sets and went to the table on the right hand side."

"I kept the envelope there," said Amit.

"I could not see that," Varsha said. "You went close to the sets, and then you ran out of the room."

"And then you stole the envelope with the money in it," said Amit, bitterly.

"No, Amit. Whatever else I may be, I am not a thief," said Varsha immediately. "I stayed hidden. I could guess that you had gone to get Dineshbhai, and would return any time. So I did not leave my hiding place. After a while, I saw the two of you come in. Dineshbhai saw the sets and left the room. You disappeared near the table for a few moments, and then you also left the room. I took that opportunity to come out of the room and left the building from the front."

Amit was silent for some time. Then he said: "You were angry with me, and wanted to spoil my reputation with Bhanubhai. You were entirely successful in your sinister plan. Why are you confessing all this to me?"

"When Bhanubhai was scolding you this morning for the damage to the sets, I was feeling happy. I was not going to say anything if the story had ended there. I had no idea then that money had also been lost. I knew that only when Bhanubhai mentioned it later. And I did not like that your name was involved in that. You see, just as I am not a thief, I know that you are not one either. No matter how much I hated you, I could not bear that you had to take the blame for the theft that someone else had committed. *Especially when I knew who had taken the money.*"

"How would you know that?" asked Amit. "You did not even see me putting the envelope on the table."

"That is why I did not realize yesterday that a theft had taken place. But when I knew about the theft this morning, I could immediately link it with something else that only I knew," said Varsha. "You see, *while I was hidden behind the cupboard, one more person had also entered the room besides Dineshbhai and you."*

"Who?" asked Amit, suddenly realizing the importance of what Varsha was saying.

"Between the time you left the room, and returned with Dineshbhai, someone else came to the room for a few seconds," continued Varsha. "I am convinced that he took the envelope."

"Who was that, Varsha?" asked Amit impatiently.

"Himanshu," said Varsha. "He came in a little after you left the room. He saw the sets. Then his eyes fell on the table. For a few seconds, he disappeared near the table, and then I saw him leave the room. I could not see what he had done when he was near the table. But I did not know what you had left on the table either. Today, when you said that you left the envelope there, which was missing when you came back with Dineshbhai, I had no doubt left in my mind that it was Himanshu who had picked up the envelope when he went near the table."

She paused for a moment to let the information sink in Amit's mind. Then she said, "Now do you understand why I am saying all this to you? If it was only the damage caused to the sets that you were being blamed for, I would have kept quiet. You deserved that scolding for being too smart. But theft was something else. I don't know about Bhanubhai, but some of the students would certainly believe that *you* stole the money. And no one would ever suspect Himanshu. I was the only one who knew the facts. I could not decide what to do. I did not like the idea that by keeping quiet, I allow Himanshu to go scot-free and you should get the bad name for the theft that you had not committed. But if I told anyone about Himanshu, I would also have to explain what I was doing, hiding behind the cupboard. After a lot of struggle with my mind, I finally decided that I will tell you everything." Her voice broke again. "Amit, you may have behaved badly with me," she said, "but I am not as mean as you think I am."

Does Varsha believe that she is helping me and that I should be grateful to her? Amit thought angrily. If she had not interfered, the play would have been staged in its full glory and I would not have left the envelope on the table and run out of the room. And after all this, she blames *my* behaviour?

He was about to say this to her; but before he could speak, he heard the familiar sound of the peace bell, and he held his words back. Varsha shut her eyes, and a tear came out of each of her eyes and rolled down her pink cheeks.

Amit kept looking at Varsha. There was complete peace outside, but Amit's mind was far from peaceful. Who would have thought that Varsha had acted like this out of spite and arrogance?

Amit had wished many times in the past that he was sitting next to Varsha, Varsha was talking to him, and he kept staring at her. He had not dreamt that his wish would be fulfilled in such circumstances.

Amit tried to understand the full impact of what Varsha had just told him. The two questions that Bhanubhai had asked Amit had both been answered unexpectedly. Now he could go to Bhanubhai, tell him the whole story, and be free from his responsibility.

What would Bhanubhai do? He would first call Varsha. Varsha would not go back on what she had told him, Amit was sure. But what reason would she give for throwing water on the sets? It would be difficult to convince anyone that it was an accident. Why was Varsha required to go to that room in the first place? And if she told him the truth, Bhanubhai and the other teachers would think very poorly of her. All the respect and popularity that she had managed to acquire so far would go down the drain.

Did Varsha think about this? Would she have realized what could happen as a result of what she had told Amit today? If she had not said anything, no one would ever have suspected her role in the damage to the sets. But no one would have suspected Himanshu either.

It was true that Varsha had caused problems for him. But she seemed to be sincerely sorry. And at the risk of her reputation, she had tried to help Amit. Amit had to admit that. His anger started to subside. The one minute of peace was working its magic on Amit.

The second bell rang after a minute, and Varsha opened her eyes. Amit had not yet come out of his thoughts. Leaving Varsha's thoughts aside for a moment, Amit steered his attention to Himanshu. He was a strange person all right, but was it possible that he was dishonest?

Suddenly, a thought struck him. He put his hand in his pocket and drew out the coupon book that Alka had given him in the morning. He examined the book closely. There were nine pages, stapled together. Very carefully, Amit straightened the staple wire using his fingernail. Then one by one, he removed the pages. Between the last two pages, little pieces of paper were clinging to the staple wire.

When the book was originally stapled, it had ten pages. Somebody had torn a page subsequently.

Varsha was silently watching what Amit was doing, and wondering what connection it could possibly have with the discussion they were having before the peace bell. Suddenly Amit thumped the bench and exclaimed in triumph, and she jumped.

"What are you doing?" she inquired.

"I should have suspected Himanshu long back," said Amit, excitedly. "He had sold this book of coupons to Alka yesterday. But he had torn a page from it. In September, a student had complained to me that he got a book with nine pages. So far, I thought that the person who prints these books was making careless mistakes, but now I know that it was Himanshu, who had torn a page before selling the book."

"And he would have sold those as loose coupons," said Varsha, quickly grasping what Amit was saying. "He would not have to account for those coupons, so he would have made two rupees for each such page that he tore."

"I don't know how many such nine-page books he has sold since September, but I presume that he must have sold many. Only two cases came to my attention, but the actual number would be much higher. Not everyone counts pages of the coupon books they buy. I've never counted pages whenever I have purchased a new book. Who knows, maybe I have also been cheated."

"That means Himanshu has the habit of cheating," said Varsha. "Yesterday, he saw the envelope with money in it, and he picked it up. Amit, when are you going to report to Bhanubhai?"

Amit thought for some time and scratched his head. "That may not be very easy," he said. "He will not like my pointing fingers at someone, unless I have evidence."

"But you do," said Varsha. "Isn't the coupon book good enough evidence?"

"As I have separated the pages, it is no longer useful evidence. I will see if any student complains of having received a nine-page coupon book next week. But that still does not prove that Himanshu had taken the money yesterday."

"I will give the evidence for that," said Varsha.

"That is not enough. Bhanubhai would ask Himanshu, and he would deny. After that, it is your word against Himanshu's. Why should the Principal believe you and not him? Don't forget that you had not *seen* Himanshu take the envelope. The envelope could have been taken by him, or by you, or by me. If you had caught him red-handed, it would have been a different story. Now, after all this time has passed, it is difficult to prove."

"Okay, we will think of something else," said Varsha. But Amit reacted immediately, "*You* don't need to think. I have been given the responsibility and I will find out a solution. As it is, you have made things very difficult for me. If you do something stupid again, and if Himanshu is alerted, my job will be impossible. Thank you for the information you have given me, but please keep out of my affairs."

This came out more vehemently than Amit had wanted. He did not want to continue the conflict with Varsha, but he felt that things would never be the same between them after what Varsha had done to him. He saw a shadow come over her face.

No further discussion could take place between them, because the bell had sounded, signaling the end of that period, and the sound of the students returning to the class was heard outside. Varsha got up with an inaudible sigh, and went back to her seat.

CHAPTER 11

Funfair

Four days passed by. Amit could not think of a satisfactory way to get evidence against Himanshu. He was sure that if he reported him to the Principal without proper evidence, the Principal would be even more annoyed. He kept an eye on Himanshu during the lunch break to see whether any student went to him to get a coupon book changed, but no such incident happened in those days.

He once went to Manibhai and asked for the register in which Manibhai had been recording the sale of coupons. As the President, Amit's request was justified, and Manibhai gave him the register. The sale of coupons from June onwards was recorded in this register.

"Can I also see last year's sale, please?" asked Amit.

"Why do you require last year's figures?" asked Manibhai.

"I want to compare the current year sale with the last year," replied Amit. Manibhai felt that this was also justified, and because last year's register was still handy, he gave it to Amit.

Amit had assumed that the sale of loose coupons would not vary very drastically from one month to the next. So if Himanshu was tearing off one page from some of the books, selling such pages as loose coupons, and not accounting for this sale, the recorded sale of loose coupons should show a decline in the recent months. Amit had to do some figure-work to calculate the numbers that he wanted, but once he had done that, he realized that his hypothesis was right. Almost every month, starting from June of last year, the recorded sale of loose coupons was about the same. In vacation months like October and November, the sale was proportionately lower. Amit saw this pattern continue till August of the current year. In September, the recorded sale of loose coupons had dipped a bit, and in the last three months, this figure had reduced considerably.

He calculated that between September and January, the sale of loose coupons was recorded about eighty rupees less than in the same period last year. This meant that Himanshu had torn off coupons worth that amount. Possibly a little more, because the number of students had increased this year, and so the sale of loose coupons should also have increased proportionately.

Amit was quite pleased with his calculation and the inference, but he felt that even this could not be regarded as solid proof against Himanshu. As days passed and the dreaded seventh February came closer, he grew more restless.

Amit found quite a change in Varsha's attitude towards him. She had been trying to draw his attention, but Amit was so preoccupied with his own problems, that he did not pay much attention to her.

The funfair was going to be on Saturday, the fourth of February. The Ninth standard had been given two stalls. Parimal and Jatin were going to manage the games stall and Vandana and Namrata the food stall. Contractor's people were coming on Saturday morning to erect the stalls.

On Friday evening, Amit was returning from the cricket field after the day's session. The days were getting longer now, and it was possible to play till fairly late in the evening. Amit reached the cycle stand at about six forty-five. As he was about to mount his bike, he saw that Varsha had come out of the school building and was running towards him.

"Are you still here?" he asked. "Everyone else from the music class seems to have left long back."

"I was waiting for you," she said. "I wanted to talk to you."

"You were waiting for me since five-thirty?" asked Amit, surprised. "What is it you want to talk to me about?"

"It's about Himanshu," she said. "I have an idea, and I wanted to discuss it with you privately."

"Varsha, didn't I dell you to leave this matter to me and not to bother your brains?" asked Amit.

"Have you thought of a plan yet?" asked Varsha.

"No."

"Then the least you can do is listen to me," said Varsha. "If you don't like my plan, don't think about it any more. But at least give me a chance to tell you my idea."

"All right. Tell me."

"You had told me that day, that if I had caught Himanshu red-handed, our task would have been easier, remember?" said Varsha. "Okay, tomorrow we are going to be at the funfair and so is Himanshu. Supposing we put bait for him tomorrow and make him steal once again?"

"Nonsense," said Amit scornfully. "Are you suggesting that I leave the money collected at the funfair lying around and wait for him to come and steal that? Sorry, I am not such a big fool. I am not going to keep any money collected from school activities out of my sight even for a minute."

"I am not suggesting money. Let's lure him with some *thing*. And not something belonging to the school either. Something belonging to us. Something belonging to *me*, if that makes you happy."

"And what do you have in mind that will attract Himanshu enough to risk stealing again?" asked Amit. "And where will you get such a thing from?"

"Do you remember you had told me that Himanshu likes to collect stamps? And I had told you that I have an excellent stamp collection?" asked Varsha. "You haven't seen my stamp collection, but if you did, you would agree with me. It is one of the largest and the most diversified collections that anyone could have seen. Himanshu would be willing to give an arm and a leg to have those stamps. I bet he hasn't even heard the names of some of the countries the stamps come from."

Amit was silent. He was beginning to see that Varsha was making sense.

"We know Himanshu has the habit of stealing whenever he gets an opportunity. He also wants to expand his stamp collection, but can't, because he is too reserved and does not mix with people," said Varsha. "He is bound to think of my album as a treasure. If he gets an opportunity to steal it, he will not miss it."

"It is not a bad idea, Varsha," said Amit, "but there is a big risk involved. We will have to keep the album away from us, if we want Himanshu to try and steal it. We would be tied up in the funfair. There is a possibility that Himanshu might succeed in stealing the album without our seeing him. If that happens, you may never get the album back."

"Himanshu will not attempt to steal during the funfair. The album is so big, that he will not be able to carry it around without attracting everybody's attention. If he tries to steal, he would do it just before leaving the funfair. We will have to be on our guard at that time." Varsha paused for a moment, and then added: "And if there is a risk involved, I am willing to take it. If this can give us a chance to catch Himanshu red-handed, and end this chapter, I am willing to take the risk."

***

The activities for the funfair started early the next morning. From the Eighth standard, the two Representatives: Himanshu and Shivangi had come. They were supervising the cleaning of the playground and the erection of stalls. Amit found Shivangi a very capable person, and her presence helped him considerably.

Amit and Varsha did not speak to each other unless it was essential. No one would be able to guess from their behaviour that they had hatched a plan that was to be implemented within hours.

The stalls were erected by the afternoon. All class teachers and the students who were going to manage the stalls had also arrived. All four Representatives handed over the stalls to the respective students and went home to get ready for the evening. For this event, the class teachers were going to take responsibility for the money collected, and were going to give the account to Manibhai on Monday morning. When an announcement to this effect was made in the assembly, Amit had thought that Bhanubhai did not want to trust him with money any more after what had happened on the Annual Day; but he found out later that this had always been the tradition. Looking to the enormity of the task of collecting money from every stall and accounting for it, this had never been handled by one individual in the past. Amit was happy, of course, that he would not have to spend time at the end of the funfair in such activities. He was going to need that time for the plan that Varsha had proposed.

At about five thirty, Amit came back to the school ground. The funfair had just begun. Other students had started coming. No parents had come yet. The atmosphere at the funfair was exhilarating, but Amit was not in the mood to enjoy the atmosphere. His mind was busy with the project that he had undertaken.

Varsha had not yet come. But Amit saw Himanshu. As usual, he was standing alone, not participating in any of the fun, waiting for the funfair to get over.

Amit decided that while he was waiting for Varsha, he might as well go round all the stalls. Ketan and Ghanshyam were with him. The three of them went to each stall. Amit had thought that the round would be a quick one, but that was not to be. The students in each stall insisted that Amit and his friends taste what the stall had to offer or play the game there. Ketan and Ghanshyam had nothing better to do, and were bent upon doing full justice to each stall. So Amit also had to spend more time at each stall than he wanted to. He kept looking at the entrance, but Varsha hadn't come yet.

Amit was quite full, having eaten at every food stall. So far he had found *pani puri* in the Fifth standard stall to be the best. Soon they reached the stall run by the girls from their class. Vandana called Amit from a distance and asked, "what would you like to have? *Bhel puri* or *ragda patties?*"

"Nothing," said Amit. "I have been eating at all stalls and I am too full."

"That's not fair. How can you eat at the other stalls and not eat at your own stall? Namrata, serve him *ragda patties.*"

Ragda was very watery. Amit mentioned this to Vandana. But he could not hear her response, as his attention had been diverted. He had just seen Varsha enter from the front entrance with Purnima, and she was carrying an enormous album.

Amit had decided that he would stay as far from Varsha as possible in the funfair, so that Himanshu would not suspect anything unusual. Thinking that Varsha would come straight to the girls' stall, he started to edge away from that stall. Right across was the stall run by the boys from his class. Amit went there. Himanshu was not very far from there.

Parimal saw him, and called him. Their stall had the horse race. "The next race is at six thirty," shouted Parimal, to make himself heard above the din. "Which horse are you betting on?"

Jatin brought his face close to Amit's ear, and whispered hoarsely, as if revealing a secret: "Horse number four is going to win."

"Okay," said Amit, taking out a rupee from his pocket and giving it to Jatin. "But if that horse does not win, I will take back my rupee from you."

The horse race was a very popular game at the funfair. A large rack in the stall had six cardboard cut-outs of horses stacked one below the other. As the race started, Jatin would throw two large dice. The first would indicate which horse would move, and the second, how many squares. The horse to reach the other end first was the winner. The game was so popular that this stall always drew the largest crowd, and once the race started all students and adults would start shouting, rooting for their horses.

There was some time before the six thirty race started, so Amit turned his attention to Varsha. She had gone to her friends, and if anybody asked her about the album, she would show the entire stamp collection. She spotted Himanshu, and started drifting towards him, dragging Purnima with her. It was not long before she captured Himanshu's attention, although she did not even look at him.

"Oh, there is Trupti," said Varsha suddenly, and waved at Trupti, calling her there.

"Hello Varsha, what are you carrying in your arms?" said Trupti, as she came near Varsha.

"My stamp collection," said Varsha. "Do you want to see it?" And before Trupti could answer, Varsha opened her album and started describing the stamps to her. She had succeeded in drawing Himanshu's attention to the album.

"But why are you carrying such a huge album to the funfair?" asked Trupti, hoping that Varsha would exempt her from seeing the entire collection.

"I am going to my cousin's place immediately after the funfair," said Varsha. "To exchange stamps with her. See this, Trupti. Have you ever heard of a nation called Liechtenstein?"

Amit came there at that time, and said, "Varsha, Bhanubhai wants to see the two of us." Then he looked at the album, as if he had just noticed it. "What is *that*?" he asked.

"My stamp collection," said Varsha. "Do you want to see it?"

"Not now," said Amit. "Bhanubhai seems to be in a hurry. But why are you carrying this big album with you? We have to work here, you know."

"Where am I going to keep this?" asked Varsha.

"The school office is open. Manibhai would be there till seven. Ask him to keep your album for you. You can't lug it with you all over the funfair."

"But surely, we will not be finished by seven," said Varsha.

"Tell Manibhai to keep it on his table when he leaves. You can collect it from the office when you are ready to leave," said Amit. He saw from the corner of his eyes that Himanshu was all ears. But he did not show that he was aware of Himanshu's presence nearby.

"All right. Trupti, I will come back in a few minutes. Don't go very far," said Varsha, and started walking towards the school building with Amit. They did not speak to each other till they entered the building. Then Amit said:

"Well done. You acted your role very well. I kept watching Himanshu, and I can tell you, he was drooling every time you displayed your stamp collection."

Varsha smiled. It was almost the same happy smile that Amit had seen so often in the beginning, but which seemed to have dried out somewhere along the line.

"Is Manibhai going to be in the office till seven, as you mentioned there?" she inquired.

"Yes. I have checked with him. The office is going to remain open till the funfair ends – in case some teachers want to use it for doing their accounts," Amit said. "We will have to go to the office before seven and hide inside after Manibhai leaves. Himanshu may come there any time after that."

Varsha went to the office and gave the album to Manibhai. "Please leave it on your table when you leave," she requested.

Both of them returned to the funfair separately: Varsha first, and Amit a few minutes later. But Amit could not enjoy the funfair very much, because he was trying to stay as close to Himanshu as possible, and Himanshu hardly moved an inch.

Parimal called him as soon as he saw Amit. "Where did you disappear? The six thirty race was over a long time back."

Amit had completely forgotten that he had placed a bet for that race. "What happened in that race?" he asked. "Did horse number four win?"

"It ended second from the bottom," said Parimal. "You are too late for the six forty-five race. The next race after that is at seven."

"Horse number four is sure to win that one," said Jatin jovially. "Give me a rupee."

"At seven, I am going to be tied up somewhere else," said Amit.

At seven, Amit left the grounds without saying anything to his friends. The funfair was at its peak at that time. Amit heard the lively music fade in the background, as he entered the school building. He went straight to the office. Manibhai was preparing to leave. The album was on the table.

Amit stood outside for a while. Then Varsha came.

"Manibhai has just left," said Amit. "Did you see Himanshu?"

"Yes," said Varsha. "Just about five minutes back when Himanshu was in the earshot, I told Purnima that I will leave the funfair at seven thirty. If Himanshu wants to attempt to take the album, he will come here before seven thirty."

"He has not seen you coming here, I hope," said Amit.

"No," said Varsha. "Now let us hide in the office."

The office was much smaller than the craft class, where Varsha had taken refuge only a few days back. There was a cupboard, and there was enough space for one person to hide behind it. The only other furniture in that room was a table and two chairs. The album lay on the table.

"Hide behind the cupboard," said Amit to Varsha. "I will try and squeeze under the table."

The table was low, and the visitor's chair was shielding Amit from being seen from outside. The room was quite dark.

Both of them stayed hidden without making any sound for about ten minutes. Amit had started feeling cramped.

Yesterday, when Varsha had proposed the plan, it had sounded good to Amit, but as minutes ticked by, Amit started to wonder whether Himanshu would be caught in their snare.

At seven twenty, he heard footsteps outside. He became alert. Soon he saw two feet near the door. After a moment's hesitation, the feet came in the room and moved towards the table. Another pause, and then they turned around and started scampering towards the door. Amit crawled out immediately, stood up, grabbed the figure running out of the door by the scruff of the neck and turned it around. He was staring at a thunderstruck face of Himanshu.

All this was so sudden for Himanshu, that he froze for a moment, and then he tried to free himself from Amit's grasp. But Amit turned out to be too strong for him.

"Himanshu," said Amit. "The album that you are carrying in your arms belongs to Varsha."

Without an argument, Himanshu gave the album to Amit. Amit put it back on the table.

"You have a despicable habit of stealing," said Amit. "You may think that no one knows about it. But I do. You were the one who had stolen the money during the Annual Day function."

"Who told you?" asked Himanshu. "You are lying. I haven't stolen the money."

"Like you didn't try to steal Varsha's album today?" asked Amit.

"Yes. And if you say anything about this to Varsha, I am going to deny it," said Himanshu. "I will tell Bhanubhai that you are trying to malign me."

"I won't need to say anything to Varsha," said Amit. He reached for the switch and switched on the light in the room. Varsha came out from behind the cupboard. It was time for one more shock for Himanshu.

"What were you doing here?" he asked.

"Waiting for you," said Amit. "We knew you would come here to steal the album. We had planned this to let you know how much we know about you. Did you suggest speaking to Bhanubhai? Let's go."

"No. I don't want to speak to Bhanubhai," said Himanshu, scared.

"But *I* want to speak to him. And if you are also present, it will make things easier for all of us," said Amit. "Do you think I will keep this to myself, after knowing what you have been doing? If I did, I would have to take the blame for the stolen money."

"I am not going to confess to having taken the money before Bhanubhai," said Himanshu. "What are you going to do about that?"

"I will take Bhanubhai to the canteen and show him the coupon books in your drawer. How many coupon books do you have there with a page missing?"

This was too much for Himanshu. Colour drained out of his face. "How do you know that?" he asked feebly.

"I know everything about you. How many such pages have you torn off so far? Forty? Fifty?"

Himanshu covered his face with both hands and nodded.

"You have cheated on every occasion. When you got the responsibility for the canteen, you swindled students to make money. On the day of the Annual Function, when you saw the envelope filled with money, you did not think of giving it to the person it belonged to. You pocketed that. Now, you made an attempt to steal Varsha's stamp collection."

"What can I do?" Himanshu shouted suddenly, taking the hands away from his face. Anger and contempt showed on his face. "I have never got anything in my life. All other boys keep getting things they want. How do you think I feel about it?" Suddenly he started sobbing. Tears ran down his cheeks. Varsha turned her face away. She couldn't bear to look at a grown up boy crying.

"Everything was fine till five years ago," Himanshu continued after some time. "But after I got a younger brother, things changed for me. Now, if anything new comes to our house, it is for my brother. I get nothing." His body heaved once again. "I thought I would use the money that I have got for buying things for myself. And I wanted to take Varsha's album, because I also wanted to have a large stamp collection."

"If you had made friends, you could also have collected as many stamps," said Amit. "It is very wrong to steal something, just because you want it too. Did you stop to think how much effort Varsha would have put in to collect so many stamps? Did you consider how she would feel if you stole it?"

Himanshu kept quiet. Only sounds of sobs could be heard.

"Himanshu," said Varsha, who had been silent all this time. "You stole the money, and Amit got blamed for it. You were present at that time. Didn't you think it wrong that somebody else should get punished for something that you have done?"

"I will return that money," said Himanshu. "I had also made about a hundred rupees selling coupons, and I will return that also. But please don't tell Bhanubhai. If he comes to know about this, I will get removed from the school, and my parents will kill me."

"Parents don't kill their children," said Amit. "They will correct your habits. I am afraid I don't have any alternative. I will have to speak to Bhanubhai. He has given me certain responsibilities, and I will have to fulfill them. But this is what I promise you. If you come with me and confess everything before Bhanubhai, I will try to convince him that you should not be removed from the school. Whether Bhanubhai will accept my recommendation, I can't say. But I will try my best."

"I won't have the courage to face Bhanubhai," said Himanshu.

"If you don't confess before him," continued Amit, "I will tell him everything I know about you. Varsha also knows quite a lot. And we will both try to make sure that you don't stay in this school."

Himanshu did not know what to say, and he kept quiet.

"On Monday, after the assembly, we will both go to the Principal's office," said Amit. "I will wait for you."

***

The Himanshu chapter was coming to a close, but Amit's restlessness had not abated. He had no idea how he would explain the damage to the sets to the Principal. It was true that Varsha had acted out of spite and caused a lot of damage. But she had felt genuinely sorry for it. She was trying her best to solve whatever problems she had created for Amit – even at the risk of losing something that was very valuable to her. He could imagine what would happen to her if he told Bhanubhai what he knew about the damage, although from Varsha's behaviour, he could not make out whether she was fully aware of the danger she was in.

On Monday morning, another thought worried him. What if Himanshu decided not to come to school? Fortunately, that worry turned out to be unfounded. Himanshu did turn up, but his face was very pale and he did not even look at Amit. Amit thought the assembly was dragging on that day. Even Bhanubhai seemed to be in a mood for a longer speech than usual, and Amit was unable to pay attention to what he was saying.

As the assembly finally ended, Bhanubhai went back to his room and all students started to file out. Amit looked at Himanshu.

"We have to go and see Bhanubhai, remember?" he asked.

There was no reply from Himanshu, but after the entire hall was vacated, he silently followed Amit to the Principal's office.

Students were always allowed to enter the Principal's office. Only they had to take his secretary's permission. When the secretary saw the President and the Secretary of the Council wanting to see the Principal, he had no hesitation in allowing the two to enter.

Bhanubhai looked up from his work, and seeing the two of them, assumed that they had come in connection with the Council work. "What is it?" he asked.

"Himanshu wants to speak to you," said Amit.

"What is it, Himanshu?" Bhanubhai asked, turning to Himanshu.

For some time, Himanshu stood silently. His face had turned black. Then suddenly, he started howling at the top of his voice.

"What is wrong with Himanshu?" asked Bhanubhai, turning to Amit in bewilderment.

"Let him speak," said Amit coolly.

Unable to understand what was going on, Bhanubhai kept turning his gaze from one student to the other, stupefied. Then Himanshu started speaking, sobbing loudly at the same time.

"I have been dishonest. On the Annual Day, I stole the money. I have also been tearing off a page from the coupon books. But please don't remove me from the school. I will not do this again."

***

When Amit returned to the classroom, the first period was about to end. Varsha looked at him, eagerness and curiosity written all over her face. Her curiosity increased as the day progressed, because twice during the day, Amit was called to the Principal's office. It was not until the end of the day, that Amit got a chance to meet her alone. Both stayed in the classroom for some time after everyone had left for the activities, and as soon as they were alone in the class, Varsha said to him, "you will have to tell me everything that happened."

"I could not have asked for better ending to this chapter," said Amit. "In the morning, Himanshu came with me. I did not have to say anything to Bhanubhai. Himanshu confessed to everything. He told him about the money that he had taken and also about the coupon books. He broke down while talking, so Bhanubhai sent him home, and asked me to repeat everything. He then called Jayaben and Himanshu's class teacher to take their views in the matter.

"At first, I thought that Bhanubhai will not allow Himanshu to continue in the school. I felt sorry, and told them what Himanshu had said about his younger brother. The three of them listened to that carefully, and then Bhanubhai telephoned Himanshu's mother and asked her to come and meet him.

"When I met Bhanubhai again in the afternoon, he told me that Himanshu's mother had come and met him and the other teachers. Bhanubhai admonished her and said that because of her carelessness, Himanshu's mental make up was getting affected. She appeared shocked, apologized profusely, and promised that she would take better care of Himanshu's needs in future. Himanshu has not been removed from the school, and after a few days' leave, he will join school again. Bhanubhai has given me strict instructions that no other student in the school should know about this. Of course, you have been so closely connected with all of this, that there was no way I could keep this from you."

Varsha was silent for a while. Then she asked: "Did Bhanubhai mention the damage to the sets?"

Amit glanced at her quickly. So she *was* worried about this, he thought. "No," he said.

"Perhaps he will forget about it," she said hopefully.

"Perhaps," said Amit. But he was not so hopeful. He knew that Bhanubhai would not forget. In the Council meeting tomorrow, this question would come up.

***

In the Council meeting the next day, only eleven Representatives were present. Himanshu was not well and was absent.

"Himanshu informed me yesterday," said Bhanubhai, addressing all Representatives, "that he finds the responsibility of Secretary too heavy, and would like to resign from that position. Today, we will have to elect a new Secretary."

Everyone was surprised. Nobody had expected that a new Secretary would have to be elected in the middle of the year. After some discussion, everyone elected Shivangi to that position unanimously.

There were not many activities planned in February, as the final exams were approaching. Pravin announced a hockey match.

After the announcement, Bhanubhai said: "When I met the Council members last, I had said very emphatically, that I did not believe that any student in our school could have the habit of stealing. Today, I regret to admit that I was wrong. A student came to my office yesterday, and made a confession. He confessed that he had taken the envelope from Dineshbhai's table on the Annual Day. He also confessed that he was dishonest in some of the other activities that he was connected with. I was so shocked to hear this, that my first reaction was to dismiss him from the school. But later, I spoke to his parents and when they assured me that this would not happen again, I decided to give him one more chance."

"Who was that student?" asked Shivangi.

"As he will continue in this school, I don't want to disclose his name," said Bhanubhai. "If we want to give him another chance, we must ensure that other students don't isolate him.

"At the same time, I would like to take back something else that I had mentioned in that meeting. I had expressed my disappointment with Amit. In that meeting, I had given him the responsibility to find out where the money had gone. I am very pleased to state that Amit has gone beyond my expectations in fulfilling that responsibility. He investigated and found out that this student had taken the money. But once he discovered that, not only did he encourage him to come to me and confess, but he also found out why this student had the habit of stealing, and tried to help him. Although this student had put Amit in a great deal of difficulty, it was Amit, who pleaded with me to give him another chance. He is a true representative of students, and we all must feel proud of the fact that he is the President of the Students Council."

A student clapped, and everyone in the hall joined in the applause. Amit's face had started to turn red again, but this time, there was a happy smile on his face too.

"Actually, I was not the only one in the investigation…" started Amit, but Bhanubhai stopped him.

"There are not many projects that a person handles entirely by himself. Taking help from others does not diminish the importance of the achievement. What really matters is that I had given a task to you, and you have fulfilled it. It was careless of you to have left the envelope lying around on that day, but I am willing to admit that you had too many things on your mind at that time, and your carelessness was temporary."

Bhanubhai became serious once again, and said: "All right. Let us now come to the other point. The damage to the set. Amit, you were going to investigate that also. Could you find out how water came to be spilled over the sets?"

The question that Amit had been dreading for a long time had finally come. He threw a quick glance at Varsha. Her face was turning red, and she was looking straight, holding her breadth.

"Yes, I have managed to get an answer to that also," said Amit, slowly. He paused for some time and then said, "I now remember very distinctly that *I* had tripped over the bucket."

The stony silence that prevailed in the hall for the next few moments was so discomforting, that Amit hastily added, "I had been going in and out of that room all the time. I clearly remember that once when I was rushing out of the room, I had stumbled over something. I was in such hurry that I did not look back to see what it was; but now I am sure that it was the bucket, and I had accidentally turned it over. I realize the extent of damage I have caused by my carelessness, and I apologize."

"You are right. Your carelessness *has* caused a lot of damage," said Bhanubhai. "But as I just said, you had temporarily lost your head at that time, because of the other tensions that you had. Looking to your extremely mature and responsible behaviour later, I intend to forget the whole incident."

Bhanubhai adjourned the meeting. As always, he left the hall first, followed by the Representatives. Only Varsha did not move. Amit went to her after everyone had left.

"Amit," Varsha looked at him and said, her voice choked with emotion. "You lied on my account."

"You may have been arrogant and uncompromising, but you have more than made up for all the trouble you created," Amit said. "I did not see the need to continue our hostility."

"It had all started with the misunderstanding at the time of the picnic," said Varsha. "But it will not happen again."

"I had tried to tell you many times before, that I had not plotted anything against you when we took the second vote for the picnic," said Amit. "In fact, I was right in my assumption that two girls had voted for Pavagadh. I happen to know who they were."

"Yes?" asked Varsha. "Who were they?"

"What difference will it make now?" said Amit. "But if you had not been so unyielding, and had come to the picnic, you would really have enjoyed it."

"I know that all of *you* did," said Varsha ruefully.

"I don't know about the others, but I had kept feeling throughout that day, that the picnic would have been more fun if you had also joined," said Amit. "I had kept missing your presence."

Varsha looked at Amit, trying to judge whether he was telling the truth.

"And I recommended Bhairavi's name for the play because she had requested for a role long back," said Amit. "I felt that new students should also get a chance to show their talents. Everyone knows about your talents."

"Sushilaben *did* explain all this to me, but at that time, I was in no mood to understand," said Varsha. "Suppose,

Amit, we hadn't quarrelled. Would you still have suggested Bhairavi's name for the play?"

Amit thought for a moment. Then he said, "Yes, I would have. But I would have first spoken to you and explained my point of view before recommending someone else. I knew how important that role was to you."

"If you had discussed it with me, I would not have felt so bad," said Varsha. "I would not have withdrawn from the chorus."

"And the chorus would have been a bigger hit with the audience," Amit added.

"Do you really think so?" asked Varsha immediately.

"There is no question of *my* thinking," said Amit. "Trupti did not sing badly, but you sing far better."

A wave of pleasure swept over Varsha's face. "Shall I tell *you* something?" she said after a while. "You are a terrific cricketer."

⬥

CHAPTER 12

Varsha's Birthday

The tension that had been prevailing between Amit and Varsha had vanished. Varsha was once again her cheerful self and laughed and joked with all her friends. Amit's worries and restlessness had also disappeared. The two of them took every opportunity to speak to each other, as if they were making up for the past two months. Amit was not sure whether the others in the class had noticed the change in their attitude towards each other. On a few occasions, when the other boys had seen them together, they had looked surprised, but no one had made any comments — at least not openly. Sometimes, Hemant and Dilip would whisper to each other when they spotted the two of them together. They would try to draw Jatin's attention to the fact that Amit was openly rebelling against the school's tradition. But Jatin's attitude towards Amit had changed completely after the cricket match, and he preferred to look the other way most of the times.

Amit had been feeling for the last few weeks, that other activities were keeping him so busy, that he was not able to devote as much time to studies, as was required. The marks that he got in one of the tests in science rudely confirmed this, and he decided to reduce his concentration on the other activities. The final exams were only a month away.

Twenty-fifth February was a special occasion for Varsha – something that did not happen more than once in a year. It was her birthday. Amit got to know of this about five days before. Varsha came to see Purnima at the end of the first period, and said, "Twenty-fifth is my birthday, and it falls on a Saturday. I want to treat everybody to an ice cream. Will you come?"

Purnima accepted the invitation, so Varsha looked at Amit. "And you?"

"Yes, if you invite me," said Amit.

"I want to invite the entire class – all the girls and all the boys."

Amit was silent for a while. He was not sure about the boys. He had heard about the boy, who had gone to Smruti's place on her birthday two years back. Everybody had teased him. Especially Jatin. After that, whether other boys would take the risk of accepting an invitation from a girl, Amit wasn't sure.

"I can't say about the other boys," he said. "I will come. Did you speak to the other boys?"

"I have started with the two of you," said Varsha. "I am going to circulate the invitation in the class," she added showing an invitation card. Behind the card were names of all students and three columns drawn: Yes, No and Will Confirm Tomorrow. Amit put a tick mark in the Yes column against his name. Purnima did the same and gave the card to the girl sitting in front of her.

By lunch, the invitation had gone around to everyone in the class. At the stroke of lunch, Varsha came to their bench again.

"Three or four girls will let me know tomorrow, the rest have confirmed," she said, and added with a tinge of disappointment, "but among the boys, no one except Amit has said Yes. More than half of them have ticked under No, and the rest haven't ticked at all."

"Are you sure the invitation has reached everyone?" asked Amit.

"Yes. I was watching," said Varsha. "Hemant for example, did not even touch the card. He read it from a distance and shook his head."

"Won't even Ghanshyam attend?" Amit asked Purnima.

"I am sure he wouldn't mind," said Purnima. "But if he hasn't said Yes, it is because he is worried about reaction from the others."

"Let me speak to him," Amit said. He took the invitation card from Varsha and put it in his pocket.

Parimal, Ghanshyam and Ketan were waiting for Amit outside the classroom. Amit asked as soon as he joined them: "Why hasn't any of you accepted Varsha's invitation?"

"You should at least have checked with us before ticking Yes against your name," Ketan admonished him. "You are in for some difficult time. Do you know, a boy named Mayur had gone to Smruti's birthday…"

"…and he had to leave the school?" Amit completed the sentence. "Yes. I have heard that story half a dozen times.

Mayur must be a chicken – forgive the pun. I am not going to leave the school, don't worry."

"Do you realize you will be the lone boy in that gathering?" asked Ketan.

"I was hoping that you will give me company," said Amit. "But you don't, I will go alone." He turned towards the other two boys and asked, "What is your problem? Why aren't you coming? Have you thought how *you* would feel if you invited people, and they didn't accept the invitation?"

Ghanshyam appeared keen to go. "If two or three boys accept, I will attend," he said.

"Me too," said Parimal.

"Listen. There are four of us. If all of us decide to attend, none of us would feel odd," said Amit. He took out the invitation card from his pocket and held it out to Ghanshyam. Ghanshyam looked at Parimal, and then ticked under Yes. Parimal did the same, and Ketan also followed suit, a bit reluctantly.

There was uproar in the canteen. Everyone in the Ninth standard was talking about the invitation. That a girl should invite boys to her birthday party was itself something to talk about. But that a boy should accept that invitation was scandalous.

Amit had queued up at the snacks counter along with his friends, when he saw Mahendra from his class.

"Mahendra, aren't you coming to Varsha's birthday party?" asked Amit.

"Of course not," said Mahendra, ridiculing the suggestion. "You can go by yourself, if you are so keen."

"I am not by myself," said Amit. "These three are coming with me."

Mahendra stared at Parimal, Ketan and Ghanshyam with great surprise.

"We are going," confirmed Parimal.

"Still," Mahendra shrugged his shoulders, "I am going to stay out of this."

After buying the snacks, the four of them went where the other boys from the class were sitting. Hemant and Dilip were waiting for Jatin to take the lead, but as Jatin did not say anything, Hemant asked Amit, "Looking forward to a fun-filled Saturday, Amit?"

"How did you find out?" asked Amit. "I thought you were too scared even to touch the invitation card."

"I did not see the card," said Hemant. "But everybody told me that you will be the lone boy among nineteen girls."

"In that case, you have been misinformed," said Amit. "Parimal, Ketan and Ghanshyam are also going to be there."

"Really?" Hemant looked at the three unbelievingly.

"Why shouldn't they?" asked Amit. "What's wrong in accepting a girl's invitation?"

"Especially Varsha's," said Dilip and nudged Jatin with his elbow. Jatin didn't speak.

"Jatin, why aren't *you* coming?" asked Amit suddenly, turning towards Jatin.

"Me?" asked Jatin, startled. "What will I do in that party?"

"What do you do in the other parties you attend?" asked Amit. "Why should the fact that it is a girl's party make it so different? If only one or two boys go, they would perhaps feel awkward. But if all boys decide to go, who is going to tease whom?"

"Varsha seems to have employed Amit as her special envoy," said Dilip. But Amit ignored the interruption and asked Jatin: "Don't you remember the fun we all had during the picnic?"

"Picnic is different," said Jatin.

"Consider that we are going on a picnic on Saturday," said Amit. "We are going after the school. The week end will have started."

"I am going to see a movie on Saturday," said Jatin. "I have already booked the ticket."

"Which movie is it?" asked Amit. Jatin mentioned the name, and Amit said: "Come on, Jatin. Getting tickets for that movie is no problem at all. Give me your ticket, and I will exchange it for any other day that you want."

Jatin looked at Amit and smiled. "Okay," he said. "If you are so insistent, I will accept the invitation for your sake."

Everyone was aghast. No one could believe what Jatin had just said. Hemant and Dilip thought that Jatin was cracking up.

Amit took out the card immediately from his pocket and gave it to Jatin. "Trust Amit to keep Varsha's invitation card close to his heart," Jatin said with a wink, but put a tick against his name.

Seeing Jatin accept the invitation, other boys also started to come forward. By the time the lunch break ended, almost all boys had given their acceptance. One boy, who had some work on that day, could not accept. Dilip was unwilling to compromise with his principles, and declined the invitation. Hemant said that he was usually tongue-tied in the presence of girls, so although he would come to have the ice cream, he would not speak with girls.

Immediately after the break, Amit gave the card with acceptance from seventeen boys to Varsha. She couldn't believe it.

"How did you manage this?" she asked incredulously. "Are you sure they have ticked themselves? Or have *you* put the ticks instead?"

"Ask them," said Amit. "I hope you have a large enough budget for thirty six ice creams."

Varsha thought for a moment, and said, "Earlier, my plan was to go to the shop near Kamati Baug and disperse after having ice cream there. But now that almost the whole class is coming, I have another thought. I will ask my father, if we can buy lunch packets also, and then spend the afternoon in Kamati Baug."

"That's a good idea. It will be like a picnic. The second one for the class."

"The first one for me. Remember?" said Varsha. "I want to make up for all the fun I missed last time."

Varsha's father agreed, and the next day, she announced the programme. Amit asked Purnima later in the day: "What gift are you girls planning to give Varsha for her birthday?"

"We hadn't thought of that," said Purnima. "I am glad you suggested it. I am sure she would like it if we gave her a good gift."

"We are thirty five of us. If we can collect two rupees from each, we will have seventy rupees to buy something for her."

"Good idea. I will start collecting from the girls today."

"Don't let Varsha know," said Amit. "I have bought a greeting card. We will ask everybody to put their names on it."

Without arousing Varsha's suspicion, Amit and Purnima collected the money from everyone and took their signatures on the card. "Trupti and you can go to buy the gift in the evening," said Amit on Friday afternoon, as he gave the boys' contribution to Purnima.

"What do you suggest we buy?" asked Purnima.

"You choose," said Amit.

The next morning, Amit came to school a little earlier than usual. Purnima had already come.

"We have purchased two music records," said Purnima, showing a gift-wrapped package to Amit. She mentioned the names of the records.

"Varsha will like that very much," said Amit.

"When shall we give her? And who will give?"

Amit thought for a while. "After the assembly, I will engage her outside the classroom for some time. You can keep the card and the gift on her seat."

A few minutes before the bell rang, Varsha entered the classroom. She was looking radiant in her new dress. The other girls immediately surrounded her. As soon as she had dealt with their onslaught, she looked around for Amit. He was waiting to catch her eye, and as their gaze met, he waved his hand to wish her. She beamed at Amit.

It was her day to sing the invocation at the assembly. After the song, she took her seat in the front row, as she always did when she sang in the assembly. Amit couldn't take his eyes off her. She looked prettier than ever before.

Amit rushed out of the assembly hall after the assembly, and waited for her in the corridor. When she finally came out, Amit called her aside and wished her for the birthday. In order to stall her for some time, he asked her the details of the arrangement for the afternoon. Varsha was a bit surprised, because they had discussed that last evening, but as she went over the plans again, Amit saw that the others from his class had filed past and were entering the classroom.

Varsha realized why Amit had detained her, as soon as she reached the class. When she saw the gift-wrapped packet on her seat, she exclaimed with joy, and hurriedly tore the wrapping off. She exclaimed once again as she saw the records.

"I wanted to get these very records, but I could not find them in the stores," she said.

Then she saw the card, and as she opened it, and found that everyone in the class had joined in wishing her, she had tears of happiness in her eyes.

Amit was watching this from a distance, and enjoying Varsha's reaction. Suddenly, his eyes fell on Jatin. To his surprise, he saw that Jatin was also watching this with interest. Although he did not show it outwardly, he was also participating in the enjoyment.

Pleasure is infectious, thought Amit. Nobody can avoid it for long.

After school, everyone went to Kamati Baug. About twelve boys and eight girls had their bikes with them. The rest walked. Varsha's father had been there yesterday to arrange for the lunch packs. The packs were ready in the shop by the time the children reached there. Soon, everyone was walking back to Kamati Baug, carrying a large pack of snacks, and licking an ice cream.

Everyone enjoyed this picnic as much as the earlier one. They spent the entire afternoon in the garden, playing games. There was no inhibition among the boys and the girls, and everyone was talking to the others freely and enjoying their company. Jatin was seen to be partial to Trupti. Although Varsha tried to behave in an impartial manner, she found herself speaking to Amit most of the time.

Around five o'clock, someone suggested a cycle race, and everybody accepted the suggestion with enthusiasm. Eight girls raced first, and Vandana won. Then the boys decided to take a big round. Amit was hoping that he would win and be able to create an impression on Varsha, but as soon as they started, he found that almost all boys were ahead of him. He finished third from the end. Jatin won very easily.

"Amit, How did you manage to lose so badly?" asked Purnima.

"He has learnt cycling only this year," said Ghanshyam.

"I have been cycling in the past," Amit corrected, "but I haven't had the same amount of practice that you do."

"I'll show you a trick," said Jatin. He mounted his bike, and went round and round with both his hands in the air. He got off, and asked Amit, "Can you do this?"

Amit could ride without touching the handle for a few minutes. Doing it for such a long time was not something he wanted to try.

"I can do it with one hand on the handle," he said.

"Big deal!" said Jatin. "Okay, if you want to ride the bike with one hand, try this." He got off the bike and told Amit,

"Keep the right hand in air, and hold the *right* side of the handle with the *left* hand."

Amit did not think this would be too difficult. He accepted this challenge in order to make up for the prestige he had lost in the race. He started riding the bike fast in a circle, and after some time, released his right hand, and grabbed the right side of the handle with his left hand. But almost immediately, he realized how difficult this was going to be. The cycle tilted a bit, and to correct that, the left hand pulled the handle in a way that it was accustomed to. Except that that tilted the bike even more in that direction, and before Amit could control it, he was on the ground with the bike.

A few boys laughed. Then two boys lifted the bike first and then helped Amit up. The wheel was at a strange angle, and someone straightened that by holding it between the two knees. Amit's knees and elbows were scratched, and his right arm was paining.

"Are you hurt?" asked Varsha.

"Oh no," said Amit, brushing dirt off his body and trying to smile. But he couldn't smile. The hand was paining very badly.

About ten minutes later, Amit saw that his arm had swollen considerably, and was throbbing. He could not bend it at the elbow. He was worried.

"Are you sure you are okay?" asked Varsha, seeing that Amit was not taking part in the conversation, and seemed quite preoccupied with his arm. She went close to Amit to inspect his arm. "My God!" she said. "Look at your arm! It is swollen!"

Jatin took a look at the arm. "Can you bend it at the elbow?" he asked trying to bend the arm.

"Don't! It is paining," cried Amit.

Jatin blew a low whistle. "I hope there is no fracture," he said.

Some more boys went close to Amit to inspect his arm. "You should go to a doctor," said Vandana.

"I'll tell you what we will do," said Jatin, taking charge of the situation. "I will take Amit's bike to his home. Parimal, you and Amit go to the doctor in a rickshaw."

"I can go to the doctor on my own," said Amit. "Let me not break up this party."

"We were going to disperse in the next ten minutes anyway," said Jatin. "And if the others want to continue with the party, please go on."

"I also want to go to the doctor's," said Varsha. "Will you come with me, Purnima?"

So Amit and Parimal went to the doctor's clinic in one rickshaw and Varsha and Purnima in another. Jatin rode his bike, and steered Amit's bike with his other hand to go to Amit's place.

Amit and Parimal went inside the doctor's room, and Varsha and Purnima sat in the waiting area outside. The doctor examined Amit's hand, and said: "There is no fracture, but the bone is dislocated at the elbow. Let me set the bone."

The relief that Amit felt on knowing that there was no fracture was short-lived. The extreme agony that he experienced in having the dislocated bone set was something that he had never known before. He couldn't bear to have anyone even touch his arm. The doctor grabbed his arm, pulled it, twisted it and bent it till the hand touched Amit's shoulder. Amit screamed violently, and tried to get up from his chair. Two strong men had to pull him back. Finally, with an audible click, the bone appeared to have got back in its original place, and almost immediately, Amit started feeling the relief.

The doctor bandaged the arm and put it inside a sling. "We will open the bandage after three weeks. Don't remove the sling till then," said he.

"Three weeks?" said Amit alarmed. "But the annual exam starts around that time."

"When does it start?" asked the doctor.

"Most probably on the twentieth of March."

"If you have taken care, we should be able to remove the bandage before that day," said the doctor. "There is not much that can be done to speed up the recovery."

When Amit came out, Varsha and Purnima were sitting outside with frightened faces. They had heard Amit's shouts.

"How is it?" asked Varsha. "Did it pain a lot?"

Parimal described the scene inside.

"It was all my fault," said Varsha, unreasonably. "It was on my birthday that you had to suffer so much."

"What does this have to do with your birthday?" said Amit immediately. "I got hurt because of my foolishness. Your birthday was tremendous fun for everyone. And me, most of all."

<hr />

— CHAPTER 13 —

Final Examinations

Without the right hand, Amit felt handicapped in almost everything that he did. He could not ride his bike and had started commuting to school in the school bus, along with Alka. Generally, this bus was restricted for use by younger children only, but Amit had got special permission from the school to use the bus. He felt very strange in the beginning, travelling with children much younger than himself, but soon he made friends with them, and started playing with them in the bus.

In most of the subjects, the syllabus had been completed and revision was going on. It was not necessary to take fresh notes in the class. But whenever it was required, other students were eager to copy their notes in Amit's notebooks. At home, Amit had started preparing for the annual exams, and he was finding it difficult to study without the use of the right hand. In subjects like maths, science and geography, Amit was used to solving sums or drawing diagrams in rough books for practice. He started using his left hand for this purpose.

The timetable for the exams was announced shortly. The exams were starting on the twentieth of March and were to continue till the month end. The result was to be announced on the twenty-fourth of April. Sushilaben was to be available in the classroom from eight to one on that day, so that students could come at any time in the morning to collect their result.

The days before the exams passed very fast. On the eighteenth, the last day of school, Amit went to the doctor after the school ended. The doctor examined his elbow, declared him fit and removed the bandage. At first, Amit found it difficult to bend the arm at the elbow, but the doctor said that the arm had become stiff because of the lack of movement, and would soon come back to normal. He asked Amit to exercise the elbow and not lift heavy loads for a few days.

By Sunday night, the arm movement was normal, and Amit was able to cycle to the school on Monday for the exams.

Amit was quite satisfied with his performance in all the papers. The Science paper was very difficult, but Amit felt that he had done well. In Maths, he was once again confident that all his answers were right. This time he had paid special attention to the method. The last paper was Social Studies, and when Amit came out of the exam hall after writing that paper, he realized that he was through with the Ninth standard.

He had mixed emotions about this. Graduating to a higher standard was, of course, an achievement that he felt happy and excited about. But at the same time, it also occurred to him that for the next two-and-a-half months, he would be away from the school and all his friends. Ghanshyam and Purnima were going to visit their grandparents in Rajkot. Parimal was also going out of town immediately after the exams. All of them were going to receive their results by post. During the long months of the vacation, he would not be able to meet any of them.

Amit waited outside the exam hall for Parimal and Ghanshyam. Both of them came out together. Both were looking relieved that the exams had ended and the vacation had started.

Parimal tossed up the history book that he was carrying and shouted, "Hurrah. End of the Ninth standard! We will be in the Tenth when we meet again!"

"I wish I could feel so confident," said Ghanshyam. "I have done so badly in Science that I would not be surprised if I have to continue in Sushilaben's class for one more year."

"I am not going to worry about the results at all," said Parimal. "We are all leaving tonight, and will only be back in the first week of June."

"We are leaving by the morning bus tomorrow," said Ghanshyam. "Amit, you have never been to Rajkot. Why don't you plan a visit during the vacation?"

Amit felt very sad at having to part with his friends. How quickly the year had passed!

He had no idea what Varsha had planned to do during the vacation. She was assigned a different classroom for the exams, and they had not met in the last ten days. Not being able to meet her also during the vacation was another depressing thought.

Perhaps Varsha had also felt the same way, because as Amit was walking to the cycle stand, he saw Varsha there. She seemed to be waiting for him. She waved at Amit and came to him.

"How were your exams?" Amit asked.

"Good," said Varsha. "And yours?"

"Mine were good too," said Amit. After a while he inquired: "What are your plans during the vacation?"

"I will be here till the results. After that, we will all go to Abu. What about you?"

"I am also planning to be here till the results. I have no plans beyond that. Perhaps I might go to Bombay," said Amit. He had stressed "I" in contrast to Varsha's "we". His father had permitted him to travel alone by train for the first time.

Amit felt like inviting Varsha to his place during the days before the result, but he could not gather the courage to ask her, and kept quiet. He was hoping that perhaps Varsha would suggest meeting. But she also kept quiet. Both stood silently for a while, and then she said, "Okay Amit, we will meet in June," and they separated.

The days seemed to be crawling. At first, Amit enjoyed the rest, but very soon he started feeling bored. He missed Parimal and Ghanshyam sorely, but even more than them, he missed Varsha. Once when Mother had to go to a wedding, Amit expressed such keenness to come along, that she was surprised. But on this occasion, he did not see Varsha. A few times, Amit went cycling to where Varsha lived, in the hope that he might run into her in the street, but each time he faced disappointment. Whenever Amit went to see a movie, he would hope that Varsha had also come to see the same movie. But she seemed to have disappeared from the surface of the earth.

Amit decided that on the day of the result, he would reach the school at eight and stay there till one. He would certainly meet Varsha when she came for her result. But unfortunately, that scheme also ran into difficulties. On the day before the result, Alka fell ill. There was nothing serious about the illness, but whenever Alka was ill, the household was always in turmoil.

"Amit," said Mother in the evening. "Why don't you leave for your school a little late tomorrow morning? I have to go to the market, Dad would have gone to the office, and there won't be anyone with Alka."

"But Mom, why do you have to go to the market tomorrow? Can't you do that on some other day?" Amit protested.

"The market is closed today, as it is a Sunday. Tuesday happens to be *amavasya*, and the market would be closed on that day also. So I have to go tomorrow," Mother said, "But I will try and be back by nine-thirty. You can leave immediately after that."

"All students would have left the school by then," said Amit disappointed.

"I would not have suggested this if Alka wasn't ill," Mother said. "I promise, I will be back by nine-thirty."

So the next morning, although Amit got dressed much earlier, he had to wait till Mother returned. Exactly at nine-thirty, he heard the sound of a rickshaw.

Amit had rushed to his bike, when he saw his mother alight from the rickshaw with heavy shopping bags. So Amit offered to carry the bags inside and keep them in the kitchen.

He placed the last bag in the kitchen, when he heard the telephone ring.

"Amit, will you please answer the phone?" Mother said from outside.

Amit was so impatient to leave by now, that he was willing to let the phone keep ringing, but then he decided to answer the phone. He picked up the receiver.

"Hello," he said.

"Amit? This is Varsha."

A tingle passed through Amit's body. Varsha had telephoned him!

This was so unexpected, that although he gurgled a reply, even he did not understand what he had said.

"Enjoying the holidays?" asked Varsha.

"Yes. No. I am feeling bored," said Amit. He tried to imagine Vasha's face at the other end of the line. He was hearing her voice after almost a month, and she seemed to be speaking in his ears, as if saying something secret.

"I called you to congratulate you," said Varsha.

"Congratulate me? For what?" asked Amit.

"Haven't you been to collect the result?"

"No. I was about to leave," said Amit. "What congratulations?"

"You have topped the class," said Varsha. "You finished three marks ahead of me."

"Really?" asked Amit, trying unsuccessfully not to sound too excited. "Who told you? Did you collect the result?"

"No. I am also about to leave. Trupti rang me a little while back. She told me."

"How did Trupti find out?" Amit asked. "Did she total everybody's marks?"

"Sushilaben had done the totaling. She was also very keen to know the ranks of her students. She told Trupti that you are first, I am second and Trupti and Ketan are third and fourth."

"You are not pulling my leg, are you?"

"Of course not. Would I pull your leg for something like this? Tell me, are you going to give me a treat?"

"Definitely," said Amit happily. "Are you leaving for school now? Let's meet at the gate. After collecting the result, I will treat you to an ice cream."

After Amit heard a click at the other end, he emitted a loud triumphant shout and jumped so wildly that the telephone also jumped with him, and then came crashing to the floor. Both Mother and Alka rushed there, looking worried.

"What happened, Amit?" asked Mother. Amit was still jumping.

"Varsha called," Amit said. "I have topped the class."

Amit's mother and sister joined in rejoicing with Amit, and congratulated him profusely. "You must call Dad and inform him," said Mother.

"You do that, please," Amit said. "I've got to go."

And he ran towards his bike.

As Amit reached the school, he saw Varsha from a distance. She was standing at the gate, waiting for him. Amit waved at her, and she waved back. A feeling of excitement ran through Amit, as he saw her after nearly a month. She was wearing a red skirt, white blouse and dark glasses, and her wavy hair was flying with the hot and dry summer wind. As always, she looked radiant.

Amit dismounted from his bike, and for some time, they stood and talked at the gate. Even if she felt disappointed at not being able to top the class, she did not show it.

After some time, they both went inside the familiar school building, and the classroom, which was soon to become a part of their history. Sushilaben was sitting in the class, apparently waiting for the two of her brightest students to come. As soon as she saw them, she congratulated both of them, and showed them their report card. Amit had got full marks in maths, and around the same or more than his expectation in the other subjects. Sushilaben also informed them that all students had passed and were promoted to the Tenth standard.

No one from their class was present at that time. Some students had already come and had gone back; the others would perhaps come later. Amit was no longer interested in waiting till one o' clock. Around eleven, he asked Varsha: "Shall we go to the same ice cream shop opposite Kamati Baug?"

Varsha agreed.

"And after the ice cream, shall we go and see a movie?" Amit ventured.

Varsha appeared to be keen, but she said, "Not today. I haven't told anyone at home, and they might get worried. I am in Baroda till the fifteenth of May. Let's meet before that. When are you going to Bombay?"

"My plans are still uncertain," said Amit. "But I am definitely here till the fifteenth."

Both started to walk towards Kamati Baug, chatting continually and pushing Amit's bike. It was very hot and the sun was beating down on them. It was a half-hour walk.

"Why don't I carry you behind me on my bike?" Amit suggested.

"Oh no, both of us will fall," said Varsha.

"I am not all that bad at cycling, you know," said Amit. After some persuasion, Varsha agreed and sat on the carrier as Amit rode the bike. He found no difficulty in riding with her sitting at the back.

They were absorbed in conversation as they approached the ice cream parlour. Suddenly, to their surprise, they saw Jatin on his bike, apparently coming from the same ice cream parlour. Behind him, on the carrier, was Trupti. Both of them had an ice cream cone in their hands, and were going towards Kamati Baug. They also saw Amit and Varsha, and all of them waved at each other.

"How Jatin has changed in the year!" said Amit. The sight of Jatin with a girl was very surprising to him.

"Haven't we *all* changed?" asked Varsha.

She was right, Amit thought. In this one year what experiences had *he* gone through! In the beginning of the year, when he had just joined the school, could he ever have imagined it?

And just as this had been a memorable year for him, Amit was sure that all his friends were going to remember the Ninth Standard at Navjivan School for a long, long time.